THE

TREASURE TRAIL

by KEITH PARK

K B P Knowledge Base Publications Ltd
Great Britain

The situations and characters in this book are totally imaginary and fictitious and bear no resemblance to any happening or real person.

Published by Knowledge Base Publications Ltd
19 Penybryn, Mountain Ash,
Mid Glamorgan CF45 3TJ

Copies are available from the Publisher.

ISBN 1-898027-00-5 Hardback

British Library Cataloguing-in-Publication Data.
A catalogue record for this book is available from the British Library.

Cover Designed by Mr Mike Kelly, Bristol

Printed in Great Britain
by Dotesios Ltd, Kennet House, Kennet Way
Trowbridge, Wiltshire BA14 8RN

INTRODUCTION.

Welcome to The Treasure Trail. Besides enjoying the story in this fast moving book, you have the chance to find two pots of treasure. Many thousands of pounds could be yours. More details on The Treasure Trail, and helpful hints are in the appendices following the story.

The first Treasure started at £6,000 and has grown with 10% of books sales added. So the purchase of this book alone adding a fraction of a penny under £1.50 to the treasure.

You are looking for a container weighing seventeen pounds, laying on the surface. It is not buried, so no digging or other damage needs to be done.

A simpler fun solution is also provided in the appendices, which allows you to get a certificate.

I hope you enjoy reading this and the other two books in the series, as much as I have enjoyed writing this one. Within these pages is all the clues, and for the first treasure a lot of help and advice.

Have fun, enjoy the book, and the places it takes you.

Keith Park

CONTENTS

TWO REAL TREASURE HUNTS

Yes. Many thousands of pounds can be yours, because you can solve the clues, that will lead you to the treasure.

START TODAY

CHAPTER ONE.

Brr-Brr...... Brr-Brr. "The phone always seems to go either when I am on the loo or in the middle of a meal," Tony said, "well I suppose I will have to leave my steak and answer the thing."

Ann chuckled, "it may only be a wrong number."

"Hello, Tony Hyatt here."

"Is that Tony Hyatt the son of John Hyatt?"

"Um-yes," I don't recognise the voice, sounds Welsh, Tony thought.

"I am Mr Patton, of Patton, Lloyd and Williams, a firm of solicitors. I am dealing with the will of a distant relation of yours."

"Oh, who is that," perhaps I have been left something, he thought.

"John Frederick Pugh, of Aberdare Mid Glamorgan. I need you to come and see me, is that possible soon?"

"How about next Monday?"

"Let me see, I can fit you in at 2 o'clock."

Ann, having overheard the appointment being made thoughtfully handed Tony a pad, and waited as he took down details of where he had to go, and how to get there.

Tony returned to the table, and continued his meal.

"Well Miss Croad, would you like to accompany me on a trip abroad, to see what someone I have never heard of has left me?"

Ann chuckled, "Wales isn't abroad!"

"You have to cross a bit of sea, and they speak another language, so it's as good as."

"I would be delighted to join you," Ann interrupted.

They had both worked in the Hotel for several years now, and as their shift patterns matched, they had become good friends. Ann often thought she would like their relationship to develop further, but was happy for now to have Tony as a friend.

The meal Tony had put on was super as usual, not surprising considering he was the hotels head chef, but they paid little attention to the food as they discussed distant relatives, possible inheritances, and played an amusing imaginative game, each outstripping the other in eccentric ideas.

CHAPTER TWO.

Tony had checked the oil and tyres, and was ready to leave on his excursion to Wales. I wonder if I should take a shovel and boots in case of snow Tony thought, as he remembered views of Wales with snow blocking roads on the TV. No, its nearly Easter, he thought, I expect all the snow has gone by now. He wanted to find out what he had been left, but the Welsh valley's did not sound an exciting place to go, he remembered from school over ten years ago, coal mines, tips, slag heaps, smog.

Although he had been abroad many times on holiday, and been to many parts of England, he had never been into Wales. He had lived and worked in North Surrey and East Berkshire only and other parts of the UK had never appealed to him.

Ann Croad, the Assistant Manager of the hotel, was a couple of years older than him, and had grown up in St Albans, Hertfordshire, but had worked in hotels in places around Britain before settling in the hotel where they both now worked.

Tony noticed Ann's arrival, struggling with a large picnic hamper.
"Got yer passport?" Tony inquired. "You look as if you're going for a week."
"Just a few necessities, so we can celebrate your inheritance."
"Champagne!"
"No, you're driving, a flask of coffee, and a few provisions I had room service knock up."

Chapter Two

They had travelled down the M4, had lunch at the services by the Severn Bridge, and was progressing towards Cardiff.
"I'm not looking forward to this," Tony admitted.
"Can't be too bad, after all we had to pay a high entry fee to get into Wales, while it's free to get out." She was of course referring to the Severn Bridge Toll.

Tony had been quite surprised, the view from the M4 had been pleasant. As he left the M4, he had seen a fairy tale castle on a hill, and having turned north on the A470, and later turned into the Cynon Valley, to find flowers by the side of the road, wild looking sheep nibbling the daffodils, and attractive scenes, not a coal mine, slag heap or tip in sight.

They arrived early in Aberdare, parked by the Leisure Complex, and looked through the huge glass windows at the various swimming pools inside.

"Should have brought my cos'y," Ann said. "We could have used those water slides."

Over an enormous foot bridge, crossing river, and road in one go, and except for the views of the mountains around, you could have been in any town in Britain.

Passing up through the pedestrianized shopping centre, they asked some children the way, and within a few minutes had found the offices of Patton, Lloyd and Williams. Although understanding the children's valley dialect had been difficult.

They entered, to hear a loud voice, "look here, how much longer do I have to wait?" said a man in a strong Welsh accent.
"Natives are restless," whispered Tony.
"Mr Patton will see you now Mr Llewellyn," said the

receptionist.
"I'm Tony Hyatt, and this is my interpreter Miss Ann Croad," Tony said. "I have a 2 o'clock appointment, so shall I come back at 3.30."
"Mr Patton was on the telephone, he is only running about 10 minutes late," said the receptionist, "and I am pleased to see you brought your interpreter, I was not sure if Mr Patton had mentioned you needed to decipher some Latin for him."
Latin, Tony thought, no one said anything about Latin. Then he noticed her smile.
"Serves you right," Ann said, and they all laughed.
Not bad these natives, Tony thought, looking at the shapely blonde, about 20 I guess, could be fun, but I bet there's a big boyo' with a huge leek somewhere, thinking of a comedian he saw sometimes on TV.

Within 10 minutes the man had left, and the call came through, "you can see Mr Patton now," the receptionist said.
"I'll wait here," Ann said.

After a minute or so, Ann was startled from her daydream of her and Tony in Welsh costumes like she had seen in a souvenir shop.
"Did you find us easily, I'm Wendy by the way."
"Well, Wendy by the way, I'm Ann, yes it was no problem, not quite what we expected Wales to be like."
"Parts of Wales are like any other parts of the UK, some good, some not so, some good people, some bad. What had you expected?"

They chatted for 20 minutes or so, in which time Ann found out a lot about Wales, and Wendy. She was 20, had been to secretarial college, was very bright, had a sense of humour that not everyone appreciated, and had split up with her boyfriend after they had argued. She had bought her own car, having recently passed her test, and he didn't see why she needed a car when he could take her everywhere she had needed to go.

"Marriage and babies maybe what most girls want, but I want to achieve something first," she had said.

When Tony reappeared Ann said, "Tony, may I introduce Wendy Lewis."

"Hi, have we met before?"

"I bet you say that to all the girls," Wendy replied.

"Well don't keep us in suspense, how much money have you been left?," Ann asked.

"It wasn't, well I suppose it was, money, well...."

"Handy you bought your interpreter," Wendy said quietly.

"Ah,... yes.., this old guy didn't believe in banks, so he hid his money, and if I can find it, I can have it.".

The girls looked at each other, how, they both wondered.

"He left me his notebook, it's full of notes he made when visiting various places, and some other notes, that Mr Patton tells me are clues."

"Oh, what fun, a Treasure Hunt," Wendy said.

"How much is the Treasure?" Ann asked.

"No one knows, we know that he had £6,000 the first time, and added to it many times, but ..."

"So I'll see you both again, possibly, when you come down again to find it," Wendy said. She had enjoyed her talk with Ann, and found them both fun.

"Um...yes, possibly .... it could be anywhere, all I know is that it is in England or Wales, and on the mainland, not on any islands."

"That doesn't help a lot," Ann said thoughtfully. "Where do we start?"

"Right," Tony said masterfully, "Wendy, you have just remembered a dentist appointment, so you had better tell Mr Patton you will be out for the rest of the day."

"Yes, sir, after all he always tells me the customer is

always right."

A few minutes later they were sitting in a cafe, Tony with a doughnut. He never could resist them.

Over the next two hours they looked together through the notebook, drove around the area, and visited the house where John Pugh had lived. The occupiers had been surprised to see him as John Pugh had died over a year before. Initially, they had been concerned that Tony would want to pull the house apart and dig up the garden, but Tony had managed to put their mind at rest for the moment, after all if it was there, he didn't want them to find it first.

"We had better get you home Wendy, before your boyfriend reports you missing," Tony said.
"No boyfriend."
I wonder if I should ask her out, he thought, problem is any date would be a major expedition.
"If you drop me on the next corner, I can get home easily from there."
"Okay, when will we see you again?" Tony asked.
"That depends on you two, please call me again when you are going to be this way."
She handed Ann a note of her name, address and both works and home telephone numbers, and Ann gave her a brochure for the hotel, and wrote both their names on the top.
"We both work funny hours. We have to work weekends but get Monday's and Tuesday's off," Ann said.
"Add my number," Tony said.
"It's okay, I can get if from the file at work."
"Bye now."
"Leave a message if I'm not in," Ann shouted out of the window as they drove away.

"Nice girl," Ann said.
"Yep."

They drove back down the valley, enjoying the scenery.
"Well I suppose we had better get back, or do you want to go anywhere else, Miss Croad?"
"Well Mr Hyatt, you can take me to dinner if you like."
"How about somewhere in Cardiff?"

CHAPTER THREE

Alister Meldrum stood scruffily, as he often did outside the barristers robing room at the Crown Court. It was a good spot to overhear all types of useful information, sometimes just gossip, other times confidential information transferred between solicitors and barristers. Sometimes this had helped him tidy away old crimes many had forgot.

"I see old Patton eventually found the guy to give the notebook to."

"Has he? I don't see how he can bill the estate for all the work he has put in on that one."

"Probably not, there was a house and other assets though, so I expect he didn't do too badly out of it."

The voices of the barristers could be heard quite clearly from this spot.

"What was in the notebook?"

"Some sort of set of clues, to the deceased's fortune he had hidden away."

"Worth much?"

"Could be a very large sum I hear, all tax free for whoever finds it. Rumour has it the chap in Wales originally had several houses, and the proceeds of these when sold formed the start, and he added to it for years and years."

Meldrum's attention was captured, tax free fortune, hidden treasure, several houses worth, but the subject changed and they went on to discuss several more topics not again mentioning the treasure.

As he heard them approaching the door he stood back.

"Excuse me sir," Meldrum said to one of the barristers, now in his full fancy dress outfit. "I happened to overhear you mention Mr Patton, do you know whether he found the man he was looking for?"

"Yes, he has."

"I still have some documents relating to his search, perhaps you could give me Mr Patton's address so I could return them," Meldrum asked.

"Sorry, but you can get it from a directory or the telephone book covering Aberdare."

"Thank you sir."

At that moment the court usher called out, "Detective Inspector Meldrum, Court 3," and Meldrum went into court.

The barristers stood watching him.

"Alister James Meldrum, never heard of him helping anyone before."

"They say he has a good clean up rate, possibly one of the best coppers in the country."

"Did you say clean up or fit up."

"Come on now, you can't win all your cases."

"You see that chap sitting over there, that's Michael Jessett, known as Mickey, only a Detective Constable, but could have been a real good copper if he hadn't mixed with Meldrum."

"Late 20's, divorced I hear, no education to speak of, yes I know him, perhaps Meldrum will make something out of him."

"As a prosecutor I see you like Meldrum, as a defender I wish the earth would open up and swallow him."

A little while later, Meldrum, having completed giving his evidence and being cross examined, approached Mickey Jessett.

"Not a bad morning's work, if I do say so myself, chalk up another one for a long holiday."

"I wasn't sure he was guilty," Mickey replied.

"Not our concern, we collect the evidence, the barristers argue the toss, and the jury decides, and if he wasn't guilty, I expect he had done several other things and got away with it, so the scales of justice will still balance."

"Don't you think we should have told the defence we knew of an alibi, that put him at another place at the time."
"Definitely not, not our job to help them, anyway I'm not sure I believe that Doctor who said he stopped to help him change his tyre."
"But ..."
"The case is over," Meldrum interrupted, "and on to the next one, but I need to get back to the nick and book a day or two off next week."
"Going anywhere, nice?"
"No, thought I might go to the west country."
"Back to the nick then."
"Yes, but I need to just call in at the reference library on the way."
They looked an odd pair as they left the court, Mickey Jessett over 6ft tall, thin and tidy, and Meldrum a few inches shorter but very large built, and scruffy in appearance. They say Alister Meldrum was an idealist when he was younger, but the job has turned him sour. Some say that he lost faith in people totally, while some others say he can see and prove evil even when it does not exist. At best, it could be said, that he has made Britain a safer place, with many criminals locked away, some for crimes they actually committed.

GETTING ORGANISED

You may find it helpful:-

1. To extract all the things you are looking for onto cards for each place.

2. Working out where all the places are on a map so as to reduce travelling.

3. To use an Ordnance Survey Route Planning map which gives you a large view of the whole of the country.

4. To decode the section in Chapter Fifteen early, so that you know which clues you absolutely need for the solution.

5. To list the items you need to keep your eyes open for.

6. To make notes on each and every visit.

7. To carry this book with you wherever you go.

The more organised you are, the more likely you are to succeed.

People who do not solve the clues will be:-

People who don't look. (Stay at home or will get round to it somewhen).

People not organised.

You have the same chance as anyone else, being well organised will give you an advantage.

CHAPTER FOUR.

Normally on a Monday morning Tony would be having a lay in, but not today, Ann would be here soon, and they were going to make a concerted effort to crack the clues in the notebook. He had even had a shave, not starting work until 11am, it was unusual for him to shave before breakfast.
Knock-Knock went the door to his flat.
"Come in, it's not locked," he called.
"Ready for our breakfast meeting?" said Ann looking around.
"Breakfast! I've had mine, but I can get you something if you like."
"Don't worry, I'll just call across to room service."

A few minutes later, breakfast had arrived, and Tony helped her eat it. Once it was cleared away they got out the notebook.
"As far as I can see," Tony said, "we are going to need to visit a lot of the places mentioned, and solve clues."
"Is there anything we can do today?"
"Yes, work out all the places, identify the clues we are looking for, and sort out a few puzzles."
"Sounds a lot, we had better get started."
"Before we do, I want to call the solicitor, Patton, to see if he can answer a few questions."
"I bet you just want to chat up Wendy," Ann chuckled. "It's gone nine so the office should be open."
Tony picked up the phone, and dialled the number. The phone rang and rang.
"Perhaps Wendy is not in and no one is answering the phone," Ann said.

"Perhaps she's in the loo, I'll try again in a few minutes."
Tony tried several times without success, so just before ten, he decided to try Wendy at home.
"I knew you just wanted Wendy's number," Ann teased.
He dialled the number.
The phone rang, and Wendy picked it up.
"Hello."
"Hi, is that you Wendy?"
"Yes."
"It's Tony Hyatt, you got a day off, I couldn't get an answer at your office?"
"Mr Patton has been shot, murdered. We arrived this morning to find police all over the place, I've only just got back home."
"When, how, who done it?" seeing Ann's look of confusion he whispered "Patton's been shot, murdered."
"Kept that guy waiting again," Ann murmured.
"No one knows anything, he went in to do some work yesterday," Wendy explained, "and when he didn't come home for tea his wife went down to the office to look for him and found the body."
"What a shock?"
"Yes, the office is a mess, paper and files everywhere, the police came in looking for clues, and went through everything making it worse. Between the mess, the papers taken by the intruder, and those taken by the police it'll be weeks before the office can re-open."
"Can I speak to her?" Ann asked, taking the phone.
"Hi, Ann here, would you like to come and visit us for a while?"
"Maybe later. I want to be available in case I can help the police."
"Okay. Keep in touch, bye for now."
Ann put the phone back on the table.
"How terrible for them all," Tony said.
"Yes, can we go out somewhere? I don't feel like looking at the notebook now," Ann asked.

"Okay, what do you want to do?"
"Let's assume you find your treasure, what will you buy?"
"A house I suppose, or if its enough my own business, a restaurant or small hotel."
"Okay, then let's go and look at what's on the market, it'll get my mind off murders," Ann said as she felt a shudder down her back.
And that is what they did. They telephoned several firms who dealt in business sales, and spent the rest of the day pretending they had won the pools and wanted to buy a hotel or restaurant. It was great fun.

The following afternoon they were again in Tony's flat, and had been working on deciphering the handwriting in the notebook, when a call came through on the intercom from the hotel reception.
"Tony, have you seen Ann?"
"Yes, she's here."
"Hi, Ann here, what's the problem?"
"A visitor for you at reception, a Wendy Lewis."
Ann turned to Tony, "Wendy's in reception."
"Can you get someone to bring her across to Tony's flat?" Ann asked.
"Yes, would you like anything from room service?"
"Doughnuts," called Tony from the other side of the room."
"You and your doughnuts," Ann laughed.

A few minutes later Wendy was at the door.
"Come in, I am pleased to see you," Ann said, "quite a surprise."
"Someone fiddled with my car, and the brakes failed, the police say it was vandalism, or something, but I thought it was connected with the murder."
"Come in, sit down," Tony said. "Are you all right?"
"Yes, the RAC got the car going, but I was frightened so I

thought I would take Ann up on her offer and visit her."
"Great, well we are pleased to see you," Tony replied.
Room service arrived at that time with a large plate of doughnuts.
Wendy laughed "You'll get fat."
"Us chefs have to look healthy, after all you wouldn't want to have a chef who didn't appear to like his own cooking."
They chatted over what had happened, Wendy told them more of the murder, and they showed her what they had done so far with the notebook.
"Not a lot of progress in a week," Wendy said.
"Well now you are here, with nothing to do, you can help," Tony replied.
"No, Wendy and me are going out, shopping, and we'll see you later."

After the two girls had gone, Tony continued on his own, trying to work out the strange handwriting of the notebook.

Perhaps if he knew some more about his dead relative it would help. He took the phone off the hook, and called reception on the intercom, being put through to the manager.
"Tony here, my own phone is out of order, can I make some private calls from the kitchen office?"
"Yes, of course you can," the manager replied.
"Thanks."
That proved a wise move, as he spent over two hours on the phone to his parents, and then phoned several other relations he had not seen for some time. All wanted to know about the treasure hunt, and the murder added even more interest. He had only just returned to his flat when the girls returned.

"Spent a fortune?" Tony asked.

"No just a few necessities," Ann replied. "But we have a problem."
"Oh, what?"
"We haven't got any spare rooms in the hotel, with the convention on, and my room is tiny."
"No problem Wendy can stay with me, my flat is big enough for two," Tony replied.
"Perhaps we could swap, I could stay in your flat, and you could have my room for a day or two," Ann suggested.
"Okay by me, but have you thought, every time a member of staff has to contact you at night, they will get told to call my flat."
"Oh," said Ann "I see what you mean."
"There isn't a problem," Tony said with a broad smile on his face, "I can use the couch, and Wendy can have my bed, I'll trust her not to molest me."
"It wasn't her molesting you I was thinking of," Ann said laughing.
"I don't want to be a problem," Wendy interrupted. "I could go back home, I'm sure I'm making more fuss than necessary, and I don't want to be a pain."
"No chance," said Tony. "Now we've got you, we're not letting you go."
"Settled," said Ann. "Wendy has your room and you use the couch.
Tony went into the main building to get some more bedding.
"You'll be okay Wendy, he's really nice, he won't try anything."
"I like him, I'm not sure I would put up too much of a struggle if he did."
They both laughed.

That evening they chatted about each others' past, their ideas, beliefs and hopes, and by bedtime they felt they each had got a far better understanding of the other.

Chapter Four

The following morning Wendy shook Tony's arm lightly.
"Hi, morning, would you like me to get breakfast?" she said.
Opening his eyes, still half asleep, he saw this gorgeous girl leaning over him, with the sun streaming through the window, and illuminating her blonde hair.
"Blimey, for a moment I thought I was dead, with an angel hovering over me," he replied.
"No one has every mistook me for an angel before," she said thoughtfully.
"No, I've woken up now."
"Don't spoil it, I was enjoying the thought of being an angel, but if I'm not, I must be a monster," she said as she jumped on top of him and then ran away.
"I'll tell Ann you've been molesting me," he said.
"She'll never believe you."
"No I don't suppose she would, oh well it'll just have to be our little secret.
At that moment she threw a cold flannel on him.
"I can see having you around is going to be fun," he said as he chased her back into the bedroom with the wet cold flannel.

CHAPTER FIVE.

Ann let herself into Tony's flat with her pass key, and could hear squeals of excitement coming from the bedroom.
"Am I disturbing you, shall I come back later?" she asked hesitantly.
"No," Wendy shouted, "come on in."
As she entered the bedroom she could see the pair of them rolling on the floor fighting over the flannel.
"Goodness children, you can have one each."
"Yes Miss Croad," Tony said, giving up the fight, and getting the wet flannel wrapped around his neck.
"Well today children, what would you like to do?"
Joining in the fun, "go to London" Wendy replied adding "Miss Croad" as an after thought.
"Okay, that okay with you Tony?"
"Yes, I can get someone to cover for me lunch time, but I will need to be back by about five."

Arrangements were quickly made, and they were soon off to London.
"Where do you want to go?" asked Tony.
"Shopping," replied Ann.
"And sightseeing," added Wendy.
"And I want to see if I can find out any more about this relation of mine John Frederick Pugh, but I haven't got a clue where to start."
"St Catherine's House," replied Wendy, "there are registers, um.. indexes of all Births, Deaths and Marriages. The Public Record Office in Chancery Lane, or for military records at Kew."
"Cor, what's it like to be brain of Britain?" Tony teased.
"Okay, lets all go to St Catherine's House, if we can find it,

and see what we can find," Ann said, "and then do some sightseeing."
"What no shopping!" Tony asked loudly.
"No, I'll let you off today. Anyway we might discover some famous Croad, or a title dormant for years I can claim."
"Not much chance of that Lady Croad," Wendy replied, "I checked Debretts, and Encyclopaedia Britannica, and there are no Croad's mentioned."
"Perhaps you should have looked under Toad," Tony said jokingly. "Did you find any Hyatt's?"
"Didn't look, it was just that Croad was such an unusual name."
"Do you know where St Catherine's House is?" Ann asked.
"10 Kingsway WC2," Wendy said, "is that any help."
"How on earth did you know that?" Tony asked.
"Oh, solicitors need lots of copy birth certificates, and other information to trace people for inheritance, so I just remembered having to type all the envelopes."

They soon arrived, and after some difficulty finding somewhere to park, reached St Catherine's House, not knowing what to expect.

There were so many people, and the index, rather than being a single index, turned out to be a collection of large books, each being an index covering three months. As there was only one of each book, some organisation of their research was necessary, but after several hours little progress had been made, and they had all had enough.

They had, however, been shown a book, by several of the people researching family trees, it was called 'Family History Knowledge UK 1992/3', and with over 1,000 pages gave so much information, including names and addresses of researchers and the work they had already done. There were also articles, and lists of record offices and much

more. They made a note of the ISBN number 1-873594-04-6, and the price of £18.95 plus £2.85 post and packing available from the Family History Club, 19 Penybryn, Mountain Ash, Mid Glamorgan CF45 3TJ.
"Mountain Ash is only a few miles from Aberdare," commented Wendy.
"I will order one of these big green bricks," Tony decided.

They still had some time to go sightseeing, and were exhausted by the time they returned to the hotel.

Ann came into Tony's flat.
"I've ordered it," Ann said, "the green brick, on my credit card."
"I didn't see a number," Tony said.
"Yes, it was 0443-478754, but if you are good I will let you see my copy. I spent £10 more than you said, and ordered the hardback copy."
"I bet there are no Croad's in it," Wendy said.
Maybe not, but with 2 parents, 4 grandparents, 8 great grandparents etc, I am sure to find some of my family tree has been done."

That evening Tony and Ann had to work, which gave Wendy a chance to study the notebook. Some of the evening she spent in Ann's office in the hotel, and by the end of the evening had built a sizable file.
"You've been busy," Ann said.
"Yes, if I can use a typewriter tomorrow I will type it all up, and make it a bit more presentable."
"Okay, I'm working in the morning, and again in the evening tomorrow but I have the afternoon off, you can leave anything you like here, as the office will be locked until the morning."
"Okay, but I had better return the notebook to Tony."

Chapter Five

The following day was similar, but Wendy also spent time with both Ann and Tony collecting information to draw details on their family trees. The three of them were getting along so well, and little did they expect the shock they were to get the following morning.

CHAPTER SIX.

At 7am, the birds were singing, but neither Wendy or Tony had stirred when there was a loud bang. The door to the flat had been hit with a sledge hammer, and five men came rushing in. Tony woke with a start, and jumped to his feet, only to be grabbed by two of the men and thrown back onto the sofa. An older man amongst the group then threw a piece of paper at him.

"Police; Detective Inspector Meldrum. That is a search warrant to turn over this place."

"Why?" Tony asked trying to get up.

"Sit down and be a good laddie, or I'll get one or two of them to thump you," Meldrum continued. "We have information that you are involved in drug trafficking. Now just stay there and let us get on with our work."

By this time Mickey Jessett had unceremoniously grabbed a sleepy Wendy by the arm and dragged her out of the bedroom.

"Look what I've found," Mickey said pushing Wendy forward.

"Had a tiff have we?" Meldrum said, "or perhaps you don't like women," he continued putting his hand on his hip and looking at Tony.

Wendy went and sat by Tony, "what's going on?" she asked.

Meldrum and all the men except Mickey Jessett were turning out drawers, and searching everything, when the cavalry arrived.

It was Ann, and a whole crowd she had rounded up, once she had been told someone was roughing Tony up. They

burst in, chefs with meat cleavers, and others with anything they had laid their hands on.
"Stand still you lot," Ann shouted.
"It's okay Ann," Tony said "they're police, and they say they have a warrant."
The crowd Ann had brought with her were annoyed, and still in the mood to sort out the intruders, but Ann persuaded them to disperse, although a few decided to wait outside just in case they were needed.

Ann looked at the piece of paper.
"Who are you?" Mickey Jessett asked Ann.
"Ann Croad, Assistant Manager of this Hotel.
"Assistant Manager eh, now in a supermarket an Assistant Manager stacks the shelves, what do you do, make the beds?" Mickey asked sarcastically.
Ann wondered whether such a person justified an answer, but with an air of contempt she replied, "the Hotel Manager has three people reporting to him, Tony the Head Chef, the Assistant Manager in charge of conference facilities and outside catering, and me, I manage the hotel."
"Oh, pardon me for speaking," Mickey said.
Ann turned to Tony.
"Shall I get a solicitor organised?"
"No, wait and see what happens," Tony replied.

After a few minutes had passed two of the men grabbed Tony and put him in a chair at the dining table. The two girls followed.
"Got you," Mickey said, slamming a small plastic bag containing white power on the table.
"I've got lots of that," Tony said. "Would you like some more?"
"You stay put," Meldrum said. "We'll find it," and shortly after they did, putting a large plastic bag on the table.
"With a little bit, you might have got away with being a user, but with all this we have got you as a dealer,"

Meldrum said.

"I'd confess," said Mickey.

"Okay, you got me," said Tony laughing.

The girls looked at each other in surprise.

"I confess, I was going to clean the fridge out today," and before he could say anything else, everything in the fridge had been removed, and opened.

"Wise guy eh?" Meldrum said.

At that moment one of the men appeared from the bedroom.

"Found the distribution chain Guv," he said.

"Who's writing is this?" Meldrum asked.

"Mine," Wendy said.

"Ah, you in it too," Mickey said, "and I thought you were just a blonde bimbo."

"That's not a distribution chain," Wendy said "look it's a family tree."

"Oh, yeah that's a new one," Mickey said interrupting.

"Yes, you see these dates, half the people have been dead for years."

"We still have the powder," Mickey replied.

"N.A.Two, C.O.Three, Sodium Hydrogen Carbonate," Tony said.

"Bloody chemist as well eh, do you make this stuff?" Mickey asked.

"No, but I could, from seaweed ash," Tony replied.

Ann burst into laughter having realised what it was, and whispered to Wendy, "Bicarbonate of Soda, used in baking and cleaning etc."

"Funny - eh, well explain this," Mickey said pointing towards bank statements in front of him, "large regular payments."

"Called salary," Tony replied.

"Not that much, you're only a cook and I don't earn that much," Mickey said.

"He needs it to support all his children," Ann broke in, "fourteen lots of maintenance to pay plus two more on the

way."
"Blimey I can see why you sleep on the couch," Mickey said.
Turning to Mickey Ann asked "away a lot from school were you, ill a lot?"
"No, why?"
"Oh, it must have been unlucky you were away the day brains were handed out."
"Why do you say that?"
"Bicarbonate of Soda, dummy."
"Oh.... it might be," Mickey said.
Ann asked "tea gentlemen," and they replied yes, she went to the intercom and ordered it.

When it arrived she gave everyone a cup leaving Mickey Jessett to last.
"Tea," she said handing him a children's feeding cup.
"What's this?" he said in astonishment.
"Tea."
"Why is it in this thing?"
"Sorry I didn't realise you could manage a big cup...."
Meldrum interrupted "Just take the top off Mickey, ignore the silly cow."
Meldrum continued. "Okay, you get away with it this time, but we may be back."

After they had left, Tony and Ann were so busy putting clothes back away, and tidying up the mess the police had left that they did not notice Wendy was sitting quietly staring at Tony.

How could I possibly like him, she thought, all those illegitimate children, just think I could have so easily been his next victim. The more she thought of it the more annoyed she became, until she could hold it in no longer.
"How could you. How could you.... all these poor girls.....

all those children," she shouted. "I liked you, I bet you thought I would be your next victim."
Tony walked over to where his bank statements were, and collected his cheque book stubs, without saying a word.

He knelt down by Wendy, kissed her on the cheek and dropped a pile of statements and stubs on her lap.
"Look, no payments, no children, Ann was just winding that wally up."
She looked, and threw her arms around his neck breaking into tears.
"So...so... sorry," she cried. "What with the murder, my car, then all this, I don't know what I think anymore."

Tony hugged her gently, saying "all right .... I understand" several times.
"Here Wendy, have some of your tea," Ann said handing her a cup.

After she had drunk some of her tea, she said she would like to go back to bed for a while and the others agreed. After they had finished clearing up they decided to look at the notebook, but couldn't find it.
Ann called quietly to Wendy, "are you awake?"
"Yes."
"Do you know where the notebook is?"
"No. It's out there I haven't got it."
They searched everywhere, but there was no sign.
"One of those coppers nicked it," Tony said.
"Then we'll report it."
"No use, they won't say they've got it, and after all they will say it is of no value anyway."
"You're sure?"
"Well that's the end of the Treasure Trail, what shall we do now?"

A few minutes later Wendy came out of the bedroom.
"I've got the centre two pages of the notebook, it fell out, and I forgot to put it back," Wendy said handing Tony the pages.
"Well how about that, we get part, and the thieving coppers have part, so no-one can find the treasure."
They were discussing what had happened, when Wendy asked Ann "can I borrow your keys to your office, I've got some of my stuff there?"
"Sure - okay," Ann said handing her the key.
After Wendy had left Tony said, "she's still very upset, do you reckon she's leaving?"
"Hope not."
They were discussing what they could do to persuade Wendy to stay, and how they could help her, when she burst in with a huge smile on her face.
"I've got two things to show you," she said in excitement.
"This is the typescript I have been working on, I've deciphered the entire notebook, and typed it all up."
"Fantastic," said Tony.
"And this," said Wendy, "is a set of enlarged photocopies I made of the notebook to help understand the handwriting."
"We can continue, but what if these coppers realise the notebook is incomplete and come back for more?" Ann asked.
"No," said Wendy, "these pages were separate, they won't notice."
"Just to be on the safe side," Tony said, "we will produce another copy and deposit at the bank, and hide the centre pages."
"File them in my office," Ann said. "After all, even I can't find anything in my filing system."
"The copy for the bank," Wendy said. "I could make it look like a legal document a conveyance or deeds."
"Would it fool them?" Tony asked.
"Yes, you could borrow money on the strength of my deposited deed."

"And I thought we needed to find the treasure," Ann laughed.

Over the next couple of days, they had a lot of fun, and totally forgot about the police raid. They had the door to the flat repaired, and planned their first visits. Everything had been prepared on Sunday night, for an expedition on Monday. They were all looking forward to finding the Old Man of Kent.

CHAPTER SEVEN.

A problem had arisen at the hotel, so Ann could not go, but she had insisted that Tony and Wendy went without her. Tony had mixed feelings about this, he wanted Ann to come, but he was also pleased to have time alone with Wendy.

"The task today is to find the Old Man of Kent," Tony reminded Wendy.
"I wonder how you can walk around the world in 80 minutes? I am sure that's what the notebook said," said Wendy.
"Perhaps it's a puzzle, it's like saying the Old Man of Kent will be there, he may be out, or dead by now."

They travelled via the M25, and A21, past Tunbridge Wells and Lamberhurst. Wendy was enthralled by the many oast houses along the road. She had never seen anything like these funny round, tall, pointed top houses before. The best being a group of these not far before they turned off onto the B2079.
"The National Pinetum at Bedgebury," Tony said, "That has to be the way in, unless you're disabled in which case it isn't."

They went through the huge gates, and parked in the car park, used the toilets, and then went on into the Pinetum.
"A sort of park is it ?," Wendy asked.
"Not sure, I think it has something to do with fir trees."
"Look there's a visitors centre," Wendy pointed out a sign.
"Okay, let's start there."

An elderly couple approached them. "Your first time here is it?" the lady asked.
"Yes," replied Wendy.
"Don't follow the signs, just go down to the lake, through the rhododendrons, and keep going and you will get to the road or directly to the visitors centre," advised the lady.
"Thank you," said Wendy, as she put her arm in Tony's and they set off down hill.

They went through parkland, past the lake briefly stopping to look at the ducks, the squirrels playing. Then the rhododendrons, all in glorious colour at this time of year, but not at their best yet, May or June being the best months. At the other end of the rhododendrons they came to a path and followed it until they got to a Y junction.
"Left or right?" Tony asked.
"Right," Wendy said.

They had not gone many yards, when Wendy pointed out to the right hand side a board amongst the trees.
"Let's see what that is," Wendy said.
"Okay, but be careful we don't want to get lost; we don't know how big this place is."

They soon got to the sign standing by an enormous tree. "It says the Old Man of Kent started growing in 1840, and was 49 metres tall, when this board was put up, and still growing."
"Oh, it's the tree," Wendy said.
"What do we do now?" asked Tony.
"Well we need to know how many men with 20mm heads and necks would it take to see over the Old Man of Kent."
"Well that's easy, you take 20mm from 1.7metres, and divide that into 49 metres," Tony said.
"Okay, we'll do that later with the calculator, just over 30 I would guess."
"Is that it?"

"No, we need to know how far round his waist it is in inches. It says his waist is 42 inches up," Wendy said.
"Oopps. No tape measure," Tony said.
"Take off your belt, and we can measure how many times, and mark the remainder and calculate it later."

That with some difficulty is what they did, and after exploring a little further, soon found the visitors centre, having passed through an area of dwarf conifers.

The visitors centre was a hive of information. They learnt that the earliest mention of Bedgebury was in AD815, in the reign of Kenwulf, King of Mercia; about the de-Bedgebury's a Norman family who lived there until 1450; and the seven generations of the Colepepper families, prominent in Stuart and Tudor politics, until.....
"That's the date we want, when the Colepepper family left," Wendy said.
"Well, make a note of it."
"Yes, sir ..... All done sir," they both chuckled.
They read on, about the next owner Sir James Hayes. It was said that his fortune had come from a wrecked Spanish galleon.

Wendy was reading a lot more, but Tony had decided to look around, and soon saw a small card guide available, complete with map.
"Around the world in 80 minutes," he called to Wendy, and then realised everyone was looking at him.

It was a marked walk that allowed you to see many of the special features of the Pinetum, with different tress of this and different countries.
"That looks like fun," Wendy said, "let's explore."
"What do we want to know?" asked Tony.

"Which port is the wishing well nearest."
"What is a port?," Tony asked. "No ships here."
"Must be the boards like we saw by the Old Man of Kent," Wendy replied. "Look it says here the Old Man of Kent is number 8."

They followed the map, down north avenue, along hills avenue to get to port one, and followed the signs from there studying different types of tress and places, visiting America, Algeria, Morocco, and China by the time they were at Port four.

In all there were 13 ports, or signs, and they ended up conveniently at the top of the hill that lead them back to the car park.
"Fantastic," said Tony. "The best day in ages."
"Well what bit did you like best?" asked Wendy.
"Oh, I don't know it was all interesting."
Wendy knew the bit she liked best. She had slipped on a bank and ended up in Tony's arms, for a moment she had thought he was going to kiss her, but people had come along the path at that moment.
"The ducks were interesting," said Tony. "Duck a l'orange."
"Oh poor little quakers."

They had, while on the trip around the world, met one of the people who looks after the Pinetum, and he had explained it was a collection of different types of conifer tress, representing 900 types, with 2,300 varieties or hybrids, and they had an ambitious expansion plan to get to 1800 types by the year 2,000. They learnt that these massive trees roots only went down about half a metre, and just outside the branches. That the volume of wood in a tree is about one third trunk, and major branches (usable timber), one third small branches and twigs, and a third roots. So that two thirds of the wood in harvested trees is wasted.

As they turned back in the car, Tony suddenly said, "do you know, I never thought of trees as living things before, but particularly amongst the Japanese Weeping Trees, when we passed under the canopies of the trees joined together, I don't think I would have been surprised if one had spoken to me."
"You mean you didn't hear them," Wendy said chuckling, "no good taking you anywhere."

That evening they told Ann all about their excursion, and all that they had learnt. They were so excited that they didn't spot her disappointment on missing out on such a good expedition.
"Will we need to go there again?" Ann asked.
"Oh, yes," they both said together, but they couldn't think of an immediate reason.

"By the way Ann," Tony asked, "what did you want the huge box from the kitchen for this morning?"
"Oh, it's late now I'll tell you about it in the morning," Ann replied as she left.

CHAPTER EIGHT.

The following morning, Tuesday; Ann and Wendy were sitting in Tony's flat trying to solve one of the puzzles. Ann was studying the page.

"It says; England and Wales go together like two parts of a well developed lady, keep your eyes open, in the valley of ferns, and near WKLB. I hope this will not extend you."

"I have looked in every guide book, and everything I can think of, but I cannot find any reference to either WKLB, or the valley of the ferns," Wendy said.

"I think it's some sort of puzzle, perhaps the bit about keeping your eyes open is the important bit," Ann replied.

"What if it was something at the Pinetum we visited yesterday, and we didn't notice?"

"Well you wanted to go back again didn't you?"

Tony arrived back, "any luck with that clue?" he asked.

"No," Ann said, "we will just need to make a note of WKLB, and the valley of the ferns, and keep our eyes open," Ann replied.

"Isn't that just what the clue said?" he asked. "By the way you were going to tell me about the big box."

"Ah, yes.... It was a bit of fun. I sent it, having glued it solid, and wrapped about 2 reels of parcel tape around it, to that daft copper, Jessett, with a little note on the outside saying he had left the enclosed evidence behind on his visit, and sending them a bill for repairing the door."

"What was in the box?" Wendy asked.

"Nothing."

"Oh," said Wendy, not really seeing the funny side.

"I wouldn't wind him up too much, or you'll start getting speeding tickets and messed about for the rest of time,"

Tony advised.
"No. I doubt if he understood. He will probably be around later asking what was supposed to be in the box."

She had hardly finished speaking when there was a knock at the door, and there they were, Detective Inspector Meldrum, and Detective Constable Jessett.
"Oh, you waited to be invited in this time," Tony said sarcastically.
"Yes, sir, I have to interview Miss Wendy Lewis, and take a statement for the South Wales Police," Meldrum said.
"Oh!" Wendy said. "Is it about what was done to my car?"
"Don't know anything about any car," Meldrum said. "Perhaps you would like to come with us down to the station?"
"No. You ask me here. I'm not going anywhere," Wendy said being surprised at just how confident and forceful she sounded.
"Not got your gang of cut throats with you today?" Mickey Jessett said turning to Ann.
Ann didn't answer him but turning to Meldrum said, "I sympathise, it really can be difficult to get good staff, and I don't suppose there is a lot of applicants to choose from."
"Enough of this," Meldrum said. "Let's get on with the statement and get back to our own work."

They asked Wendy about her movements on the afternoon Mr Patton was shot, whether she had ever used or owned a gun, and of anyone who could vouch for her at the time in question.

"Now the important question," Meldrum said. "You were heard to threaten Patton about a week before he was murdered."
"Not me," she replied.

Jessett reading from his notebook said "If you lay your hands on me again, I'll do something to make sure you never do it again, so be warned."
"I didn't, ah yes.... um, it wasn't me exactly, I was reading a piece from a divorce petition. It was a bit of fun. Mr Patton wasn't even in the room."
"Right, I've noted that," Mickey Jessett said. "Denied until confronted with the facts, and then came up with an excuse."
"So you are saying you didn't kill him I suppose," Meldrum said.
"Of course I didn't, I liked him."
"I see, there was something going on between you and your boss," Meldrum snapped.
"No, nothing like that."
"Well what was it like?"
"I'm not answering any more of your silly questions, so just leave me alone."
"Time to go Inspector," Ann said, "and take your wooden top with you."
"There is another matter," Mickey Jessett said looking at Ann. "Wasting police time.... with that box."
"Good job I didn't write, open the other end on both ends, or you would still be there," she mimicked turning a box over and reading and turning over again continuously.
"I've had enough of you, just don't walk down any dark alleys on your own."
Turning to Meldrum Ann said, "quick arrest him, he's threatening to do me in."
"No, I didn't understand it as that," Meldrum replied. "He was just giving you the standard advice we give to all ladies, it is unwise to walk down dark alleys on your own."

They packed up their papers and left, but Tony kept an eye on them to make sure they didn't take anything else as well.

"You were quiet," Ann said to Tony.

"You didn't need any help, you were annoying him enough on your own."

Wendy broke in, "do you think I'm a suspect?"

"Looks like it," Tony said. "But there are probably hundreds of suspects."

"I hope they don't come back again."

"Come on, it's only 9.45, so lets go out on another expedition, where would you like to go?"

"My choice," said Ann. "How about the place with the Motor Museum, House, Gardens, small animals and wildfowl."

"Yes, I want to solve the riddle of the sphinxes," Tony said.

CHAPTER NINE.

"Bentley here we come," Wendy said. "Ann, why don't you read out the clues we are looking for."
"Okay, we want to know the colour of the cat on the roof of the tea room."
"Hopefully it's there today," Wendy broke in.
"Probably painted on the roof or something," Tony said thoughtfully.

M25, M23 to junction 10, A262 to East Grinstead, and A22 down to just the other side of Uckfield, past the A26 junction and hopefully Bentley will be signposted on the right.
"What are the other clues Ann?"
"We want to know how many sphinxes there are; the date on early driving licences; how many white octagons on a floor; and the number of paintings of birds in the house by an artist.... Oh; and where a firm that sold cars were based."
"Quite a lot, but it sounds just a case of searching," Wendy said.
"Except for the thing about the sphinxes, in their case there is a rhyme or puzzle it says; If sphinxes in total half a dozen there are, ahead you go, less you turn left, more you turn right."
"Well that's clear as mud. I could do with a doughnut about now."
"Tony! You and your doughnuts," Ann said.

They didn't have any problem finding Bentley, and Tony and Ann made immediately for the tea room.
"Well we have seen the cat, and noted its colour," Ann said watching Tony eating a huge doughnut. "Where shall we

start?"
At that moment Wendy came in.
"Look I've got a guide book from the gift shop, it has a map, and look," she said in excitement, "on this page it shows a plan of the gardens, and there are the sphinx, in the sphinx garden."
Ann looked, "I wonder if there are any more besides these," she said showing it to Tony.
"Maybe, but I wouldn't have thought so, seems all very tidy and well organised."
"Look here," Ann said pointing to the page next to the garden plan, this photograph shows a floor with a pattern on it, and look it has octagons."

Having looked through the rest of the guide book, they decided to start with the small animals opposite the tea room, then look around the motor museum, before going to the house and gardens. This then left the miniature steam railway, and bird gardens until last.

Wendy really liked one of the rabbits in the small animals section, and got quite annoyed at Tony when he mentioned that it would taste good.
"How could you.... How could you!," she had exclaimed, "even think of taking his little fur coat off, let alone murdering and eating him."

He had made it worse by pointing out that the flavour improved if you cut their throats and let them hang a while before cooking them.

By the time they reached the motor museum, Wendy was not speaking to Tony, but that didn't last long, and she soon had forgotten all about rabbits. Enthralled at the wide range of cars on display, by the time they came to an impressive sports car, she was imagining driving it with Tony, with her long blonde hair behind in the wind.

"Over here," Ann shouted. "Look in this case, old driving licences."
"And over here on the wall a poster," Tony said. "Pope & Co, sole agents for Mitchell Motors, cor.... look at the area they covered."
They made a note of the date of the Motor Car Act on the top of the licences, and where Pope & Co had their base.
"Aren't we doing well," Wendy commented.
"Seems too easy, doesn't it?"
"Maybe there is a trick, better keep our eyes open," Tony said cautiously.

Having spent some more time looking around the vehicles, bicycles and other items in the motor museum, they went on to the house. The very first room they entered, had the floor with octagons, and they were easy to count. In fact it was a very interesting floor as the marble had fossils in it.
"Birds.... Birds everywhere," Tony exclaimed. The walls were covered in paintings.

He was part way through counting them when he noticed the girls chuckling and looking at him.
"I've lost count now, what are you two giggling about anyway?"
"Oh, nothing, you count them, and we will tell you if you have got it right," Ann said waving him on.
"How will you know?" he said in astonishment.
"Fancy a game of ping pong," Wendy said, showing him a bat giving tourist information about the room. "A total of ... in the house by Philip Rickman."

They looked around the rest of the house, Tony said he would like a solitaire table like the one on display. Ann said she could really do with the giant book tables, with lots of storage inside, and Wendy said she would make do with the house.

On leaving the house they went into the gardens. The sphinx garden being the first. They could hear peacocks, but could not see any. The gardens were divided up by large yew box hedges, they varied from the rose garden, to one with few plants, but fitted with a large T shaped goldfish pool.
"I suppose you would eat them as well," Wendy said.

Tony didn't answer, he was preoccupied with the kitchen garden, which although now used for propagating plants for the gardens, would once have been full of vegetables. He explained to them the advantages of a walled garden, and how the seasons for vegetables could be extended, and the range of available vegetables and fruit widened. They then went back out carefully looking in each garden for more sphinx, and past the house. The railway and children's playground was ahead, and the path to the wildfowl reserve was to the left.

"Quick, Quick," said Tony, "let's go and see the ducks."
"Shouldn't that be Quack Quack," laughed Ann.
And off they went, through the entrance, turning right along the side of a long pool, with the wide variety of wildfowl from around the world, overhanging trees, it was a romantic setting, and both girls minds turned to ideas of romance, but Tony was totally engrossed in the wildfowl.
"I wonder if each type tastes different," he said staying clear of Wendy in case she liked ducks as much as rabbits.
"You're always thinking of your stomach," Ann said teasing, and slipping her arm into his.
"Those little fluffy ones, are probably the same size as quail."
Ann wrinkled up her nose, "two thin budgies on a plate. Quail is a waste of time."
"Okay, but how about one of these black swans?"
At that moment the swan came hissing towards him, just as if he understood what was being said.

Wendy was about to run, when Tony caught her arm, "they're territorial, and he's just showing off, telling us to keep off his territory, he won't attack." Tony reassured her.

Talk then turned to the variety, colour, the brightness of the males as opposed to the females, and such variety on show. At the end of the lake, they turned a corner to see more varieties in cages, some making a lot of noise.
"They're telling all their friends, you want to eat them," Wendy said. "You watch out there'll be an ambush around the next corner."

They spent some time looking at all the varieties of wildfowl, and reading all the boards on display. They learnt that there were over 100 varieties out of the total of 147 species in the grounds, about the successful breeding programmes with rare birds, and that the origin of wildfowl dated back 80 million years, with the first domesticated one being the Greylag Goose 4,500 years ago.
"About as old as you Tony," Ann said and being tickled until she admitted she had meant herself.

Having been through the wildfowl reserve, and past the main lake, complete with island and covered viewing platform on legs in the lake, they left by a small gate making their way back through the gardens.

"Well did you keep your eyes open?" Ann asked as they stopped to note down all they had discovered. "Do you children want to play on the playground?"
"No Miss Croad," Wendy replied. She was used to this game now. "But I would like to look around that building over there," pointing to an exhibition centre, often used by school parties, but having several interesting displays.

"I have a problem," Wendy said thoughtfully. "I want to go around it all again, but they will be closing soon."

"We can always come back again," Tony said.
But Ann hoped that if they came again it would just be her and Tony, and was beginning to get just a little jealous of Wendy's attention from Tony.

It didn't last, and by the time they got home, they were all looking forward to visiting Bentley again.
"Tomorrow I'm going to talk seriously to you Wendy," Tony said as she went into the bedroom and he settled down on the couch.
What about, Wendy wondered.

CHAPTER TEN.

Brr...Brr...Brr...Brr. Tony was wakened by the telephone.
"Blimey, it's 9.15," he said although there was no one but him in the room.
"Hello. Tony Hyatt here."
"Mr Hyatt, I have some information that is to your advantage, we need to meet." Another inheritance Tony thought.
"Okay, when and where?"
"Can you meet me outside the Tate Gallery, on the Albert Dock, Liverpool next Monday... say 2pm?"
"Um.. I suppose I can."
"Good," and the caller hung up before he could get any more information.
Could it be a joke, he wondered, but he noted it down before he forgot.

Well he had to go up north to solve some of the clues, in fact the ones on the centre pages of the book, and next Monday and Tuesday was as good as anywhen.

He called through to reception on the intercom, and got put through to Ann's office.
"Hi, would you like to have a couple of days away up north next Monday and Tuesday."
"Yes.. Um.. Why?"
"I had a weird phone call, I will tell you about later, when are you off today?"
"I'm working most of today, but I could pop over for an hour about four this afternoon."
"Okay."
"While I think of it Jeanette Wilson has gone off with her latest boyfriend, little idiot, she's only just 17, so I need

another receptionist. Do you think Wendy would be interested?"
"Don't know, you could always ask."
"Okay, I'll come across in a while, but don't say anything, and I wouldn't mention the trip up north yet."

A little while later Wendy was up, and they had nearly finished their late breakfast when Ann arrived. She quickly filled in Wendy on the vacancy that had arisen.
"Little idiot, only knew him two weeks," Ann said.
"Oh. Sounds so romantic," Wendy said, thinking of Tony.
"Are you interested in a job, even if only for a while?"
"Yes, sure, I can't stay here permanently without one."
"Okay, well you can have Jeanette's flat, two doors along, it's not quite as big as this but better than a room in the main hotel."
"Didn't you want it?" Wendy asked. "I could have your little room."
"No, I have to be on call nights, and I wouldn't want to have to cross to the hotel in the dark on my own."
"Congratulations," Tony said. "How about a celebration, you can make us a meal."
"Me, cook," Wendy said in surprise. "Last time I tried, the meat was like a very tough pair of trainers."
"Never tried trainers," Ann interrupted.
"Come on, I'll help," Tony said. "Let's plan something new for you."
"That won't be difficult."
"I have to run," said Ann. "Come and see me later, I have to pop down the town now," but didn't actually make a move.
"It'll all go wrong," Wendy said.
"Let me tell you what happened at one dinner party I went to," Tony said. "The guy had cooked the meal and we had two girls there. They were showing off their latest aerobics exercises, and one was laying on the ground with her feet

in the air. In he came with the courgettes, piping hot, didn't expect to see anyone on the ground."
"Well you wouldn't," Wendy said.
"Over he went, and the hot courgettes, went down or should I say up her skirt."
"Was she hurt?"
"Not badly," Tony said starting to laugh, "but she didn't half demonstrate a lot of aerobic exercises I hadn't seen before."
Wendy was laughing too, and they all laughed so much that they had tears running down their faces.

Ann had heard it before, but it still made her laugh.
"Do you want to come down town to the cash and carry?" Ann asked Wendy.
"Okay."

They were coming out of the cash and carry, with two fully loaded trolleys, and on their way back to the car, when they saw Mickey Jessett ahead, with two police officers in uniform.

As they approached, he used a strange witch like voice and mimed saying "a little bit of crows foot, eh.. eh.. eh.. a bit of toad, eh.. and we have Croad. Another witch is born."
"Just ignore him," Wendy said.

They had loaded the car, when across came the uniformed police with Mickey a couple of yards behind.
"See your licence?" the fatter one demanded.
"Mine," Ann said in astonishment.
"Yes and your certificate of insurance, and while we're at it we'll just check your car out, especially the tyres."

Luckily she had put new tyres on only a month before, and

they could not find anything wrong with the car.
"You have seven days to produce your documents," the thin one said handing her a piece of paper.
"I'll get him," Ann said to Wendy, "you see if I don't."

Later that day, in the High Street, Mickey Jessett and another Detective Constable sat in their car, trying their best to look invisible.
"Isn't that the guy who's flat we raided?" the other man said as he pointed to Tony and Wendy going into the butchers.
"Yep, that reminds me I played a good trick on that witch this morning," and he went on to explain what had happened at the cash and carry.
"How reliable was the tip off that the jewellers was going to get done Mickey?"
"Don't know, it was an anonymous typed note left for me on the station counter when they were busy."
"Look down there, quick Mickey, we can catch him."
Mickey jumped out of the car and ran as fast as he could down the High Street. A person had come out of the building society with a mask on, and holding a bag, running first towards them, and then turning and running down a side street towards the canal.

Mickey chasing, as fast as he could, down the lane and along the tow path of the canal.
"Must keep going," he said as he pushed the wet grass and plants aside as he ran and splashed through muddy puddles.
"He can't be far ahead now," so he kept going. He could see a police car ahead on a bridge. We have him trapped, he thought, but I want the credit, so I must catch him before he gets to the bridge.

He didn't catch him up, and when he got to the bridge he was totally out of breath, his usual tidy appearance had changed to a person covered in weeds, and wet mud up to

his knees.
"Stop Mickey," the constable shouted. "There was no holdup just some clown in a mask."
"What....," he was still out of breath, "where did he go anyway?"
"Dono, probably hid in the long grass or something, anyway there is nothing to charge him for if you do catch him."

At that moment Ann came along in her car.
"Excuse me," she said. "Where do I have to produce these documents?"
"Any police station," Mickey replied. He was not interested in her at this time.
The police car had gone on, leaving the dishevelled Mickey in the lane.

Ann started to drive off, and then stopped. "Do you want a lift back to town?"
"Yes... Um... Please," Mickey replied.
"Okay, but don't get my car dirty, you can sit on newspaper."
Mickey appreciated the lift, but was too embarrassed to thank her when he got out.
"I should take your trunks next time you fancy a splash in the canal," Ann shouted as she drove off.

Back at the flat, Tony and Wendy had begun to prepare the meal.
"Guaranteed to be tender," Tony told her.
They had cut parsnips, carrots, and celery into strips and put them in the bottom of a large casserole dish. Placing a pound of venison, diced prime shoulder, on top, adding some chopped mushrooms, salt and ground black pepper, a handful of sultanas, "to add a little sweetness," Tony explained.

"Onion next," Tony said.
"Must we, I don't like onions."
"Do you like pickled onions?"
"Oh, yes that's different."
"Then we'll use a few pickled onions."
They chopped up 4 pickled onions and added them and a splash or two of Malibu, plus about a quarter of a pint of cider, "to stop it drying out too much," Tony explained. They then poured over a can of red wine sauce.
"This is cheating of course," Tony told her. "We really should have made the sauce."
It was by this time, 4.30pm, but the oven had been put on to warm up earlier.
"Gas 4, um... 180C or 350F on this electric cooker," Tony told her.
"How long for?"
"One and a half hours, then stir, and leave for another hour."
"So that means dinner's at 7pm."
"Yes, I'll get someone to cover for me for a while and come back over then."
Tony explained how to cook the potatoes and how to prepare and cook the mange tout.
"I've never eaten pea pods before," Wendy said looking at the mange tout.

At just after 7.30 Tony had come back over.
"I can manage about an hour, but I may have to go if they need me urgently," he explained.
The meal was giving off an aroma that made them both hungry, when Ann came in waving a bottle of expensive looking wine.
"Can you keep an eye on the time?" Ann said looking at Wendy, "I have to be back by about 8.15."
"Sure," she replied.

Serving up the venison, and vegetables together with saute

potatoes and boiled pea pods, they told Ann of the chase they had witnessed in the High Street. Ann told them of the view at the bridge, and giving Mickey a lift back into town. "Now you're moving out to a flat of your own, I can get my flat decorated," Tony said, "and yeah, I can sleep in your bed, and you on your sofa," they all laughed.

While the girls washed up, Tony had a good look at several maps, some route planning maps, and some detailed atlases, how could he organise all these visits.

As Ann left she turned back, taking a mask out of her bag, "know any children that would like a mask?" she asked with a grin.

The other two looked at each other in amazement.

RAISE MONEY FOR A LOCAL CHARITY

Yes, you can, either on your own or with others, organise an event to raise a substantial sum for your chosen charity.

Options:-

Form a Local Treasure Trail Club (APP 5).

OR

Organise a special event; Treasure Trail, Murder Mystery etc
(Some help may be available).

OR

A talk on a subject. The Author of these books will provide talks, (without charge); on Family History, Tracing Your Family Tree, or on the Treasure Trail concept, clubs etc, or on becoming an Author.

OR

Your own idea.

Why not write to either the:-

Federation of Treasure Trail Clubs
The Family History Club of Great Britain

or

The Author, Keith Park
c/o Knowledge Base Publications Ltd
19 Penybryn, Mountain Ash
Mid Glamorgan CF45 3TJ

with your ideas and some possible dates.

CHAPTER ELEVEN.

By Sunday morning Wendy had settled into her flat, and new job, but her shift pattern had meant she had seen very little of Tony. Ann had told her of their planned excursion to the North for two days, and she hoped to spend some time with them both, but particularly Tony on this Sunday morning.

She knocked on Tony's door.
"Come on in, it's open."
As she opened the door she could see Tony on his hands and knees peeping around from behind the sofa, and around the other side laughing and looking at him was a baby dressed totally in blue.
"Boo," said Tony to the baby, creating a shriek of excitement. "Ah... Wendy, you don't need to knock, just use your key." But Wendy hadn't liked to just walk in although she still had a key to his flat.

Tony scooped the baby up, put it under his arm, head forward, feet kicking furiously behind and came across to her.
"This is Aaron," Tony said, handing her the baby.
Wendy had not had much to do with babies, and held it away from her quite rigid.
"Da Da....Da Da," the baby said putting his arms out towards Tony.
Tony grabbed it by the feet, tipping it upside down to shrieks of excitement and more "Da...Da's."

Tony put the baby on the sofa, and was giving it a little tickle, but Wendy was confused, a little left out;

"I'll come back later," she said, opening the door.
At that moment a slim, very attractive brunette, wearing what looked like the most expensive designer clothes available, that really presented her figure to its full, came flowing into the room, totally ignoring Wendy.
"You are a darling Tony," she said planting a kiss on his cheek. "How's mummy's little angel?" and before anyone could answer she had picked up the baby and put it up to her shoulder and was walking out.

Tony waved to the baby, which waved back.
"Da Da... Da Da," it shrieked.
Having left, the lady as an afterthought turned back,
"Hi, I'm Monica," she said. "You must be Wendy, I've heard a lot about you, Tony's latest I hear. He'd make a good father, super with kids, I can recommend him."
There wasn't time for Wendy to think, let alone answer, before she was gone.

Wendy looked out of the door.
"Who was that ?" Wendy asked.
"Monica," Tony replied crossing over behind her and putting his arms around her waist.
His latest, he hadn't realised, but he hoped Wendy was.
"No," Wendy said, "the baby!"
"Um... Aaron, it's Monica's baby," Tony replied. "Now what do you want?"

Boy or girl she thought, I don't want a baby, and pulling free from him and crossing to the sofa, she said "No, not me, I don't want a baby.... You said you didn't have any children."
She looked quite upset, and was getting quite annoyed at the idea that Tony had lied to her before. Tony walked quickly across, and with one hand behind her back and the other beneath her knees he scooped her up.
"Put me down.....put me down," she was not amused, but

Tony was laughing and carried her in and dumped her on the bed.

"Got you," he said, grabbing both of her hands and holding them above her head.

"No, don't, get away..... leave me alone," she said.

He just transferred both of her hands to one of his, and stroking his chin he said thoughtfully, "now what shall I do with you?"

Wendy was getting frightened now, she liked Tony, but he had been so gentle up to now. How could she have been so wrong about him, what would he do next.

"Let me go....please," she said struggling.

"Not until you say sorry, or shall I give you a tickle?"

"Let me go," she cried, and as soon as tears started to appear in her eyes Tony let go.

"Sorry," he said, "I was just playing, I didn't mean to hurt you."

"You lied to me, you said you didn't have any children," she said sitting up and hugging her knees.

"Aaron's not mine. Monica is the Manager's daughter, and when she wants to have a drink in the bar with her father, she leaves Aaron with me," and smiling he added, "but only on condition I don't eat him."

"But he called you Da Da."

"I see you haven't had much to do with babies, they call everyone Da Da at that age."

Should she believe him, she would like to.

"Who's the father?"

"Oh, Monica married an Earl, lives on a huge country estate.... You don't believe me, do you?"

"I'd like to."

Tony scooped her up again and carried her back into the lounge, and going to the intercom with her still in his arms he awkwardly pushed the buttons, and was put through to the Manager.

"Hi, Tony here, I have a suspicious person here, could you tell her who Monica and Aaron are."

"Hello Wendy," the Manager said. "Monica is my daughter and Aaron my grandson."
"Can you confirm I'm not the father," Tony asked.
"Oh, I see," the Manager said. "I see what you mean by suspicious now. No Wendy, Tony is not Aaron's father, although sometimes I wish he was."
"Thanks," Tony said turning off the intercom. "Now do you believe me?"
"Well.... I suppose so," she said now feeling an idiot. "How did he know it was me, I didn't think he even knew who I was."
"To you it looks like a large hotel, but its really a very small place with lots of gossip."
"Oh... I didn't realise."
"Oh... yes, I'm sure there are all types of stories by now. I am sure everyone except us knows the detail of the steamy nights of passion."
"There haven't been any."
"Shush... not so loud. Do you want to spoil my reputation?"
She hugged him, and he lowered her legs to the ground.
"Sorry for doubting you," she said quietly. "I'm always having to say sorry, aren't I?"
"And I'm sorry for frightening you in the bedroom, I didn't realise you were so upset."
They hugged for some minutes until there was a knock on the door.

Wendy answered the door. "Hi Ann, heard about our steamy nights of passion?"
"Oh, you've heard the gossip.... just ignore it, and they will soon move on to talking about someone else."
"Did it happen to you?" Wendy asked Ann.
"Yep, but not about Tony. Everyone imagined I must be having an affair with the Manager in order to have got the job."
"Well....."

"Of course not," and then laughing she said, "of course that means he's available if you're interested." They all laughed.

Ann made a point of leaving Tony and Wendy together on Sunday, as she knew she would have him for two days. Two days she had been looking forward to. Luckily Wendy's roster meant she would be working. She had known Tony for so long, and although he had had several girlfriends, Ann had never been more than a little bit jealous, but Wendy, living in the hotel, so pretty, and often looking seductive in the black slinky trousers, with long blonde hair hanging loose, she couldn't blame Tony for being attracted to her, and above all, he was her friend. She wanted him to be happy. Secretly, however, she hoped that one day she would be his, even if only for a short time.

The following morning Tony was prepared, he had the car ready, and the route worked out when Ann arrived.
"Looking forward to a couple of days away?" Tony asked.
"Yes, but I bet you wish Wendy could come to," she hadn't meant to say that, but it just slipped out.
"Yes, and no," Tony replied. "I really do enjoy our time together Ann, and I feel sometimes I don't give you um... um.... enough attention when Wendy is around."
"It's okay, I'm not complaining."
"Come on, let's make this a couple of real fun days."
"Sure," she said, thinking she would rather make it a couple of romantic days.

They took the M25, at the wrong time of day, and got caught in a jam, and then the M1 never a pleasant road, the M6 and arrived in Liverpool at 1.30pm.

It didn't take them long to find the Tate Gallery, located between the sea and the Albert Dock.

"You don't know where, or who we have got to meet?" Ann asked.

"Nothing."

Tony stood outside, with a card containing his name, but insisted Ann went inside, as there was a very cold wind that made you feel you were frozen to the spot. 2pm came, then 2.30 and 3pm.

"No show?" Ann said coming out again.

"No, must have been a hoax."

"Well, what do you want to do now?"

"Get defrosted, look there's a shopping parade on the island bit," and they made their way there, looking around the stalls, barrel displays, and Tony brought Ann a white long furred teddy.

"Just in case I don't give you enough attention," Tony said, "something to cuddle."

"I'd rather have your cuddles."

He pretended to creak at all his joints.

"The ice man is coming," and he put his arms stiffly around her.

"Are you still cold?"

"Freezing, let's get moving, where do you want to get to tonight?"

"How about York?"

But before leaving for York they had a quick look around the centre of Liverpool, and visited a shopping centre with statues of the Beatles. It stood where the hall they originally played in had stood.

That night they stayed at a bed and breakfast place, at one Moorland Road, York. It was a pretty house, with the front and side covered in coloured ivy, and having a neat box hedge at the front.

"Edwardian," Ann said.

"Yes, probably, but as long as their central heating works I will be happy."

That evening they went out to dinner in York, but was not late returning to Moorland Road.
"Makes a change from the hotel," Ann said. "Warm and homely, if you know what I mean."

The following morning, having had breakfast and settled the bill for the rooms, they went to explore York.
"Only one clue here," said Ann.
"Yep, but its not easy. I'll read it out; do not cross the river, from the small part of the old town, and plan to have an alcohol drink with the dusty nuns. Go through the wall, but not on top, having passed several book shops, proceed to the mount, and then left into a road that reminds you of a damaged Scottish Highland house, travel about 750 metres and turn right. The nearest of the 4 main points of the compass is the reference point."
"The smallest part of the old town is easy, as it was a walled town divided by a river. There happens to be about five roads that go through the old wall, where do we start?"
"What about the dusty nun?" Tony asked.
"Could be a pub!"

It didn't turn out to be as difficult to find as they expected, having picked up some tourist leaflets.
"Make a note, the reference point equals .....," Tony said.
"Its done," Ann said, interrupting him.

Having completed this, they visited a few other tourist places, including a crypt under the Minster, before going on to Newcastle.
"We had better be quick here," Ann said. "We used up so much time in York, that it will be late tonight before we get home."
"Okay, what's the clue?"

"It says; there is a park, and in the park is a lake, and in the lake is an island. For the crow, cheers to the south and teeth to the north, but which way is the rick-store, let's call it the new-direction."

They soon found the lake in Leazes Park, with Newcastle United's football club to the south.
"Cheers must be the football club," Ann said.
"Okay, what's a rick-store, and why does it specify for the crow?"

They had soon solved the clue, and noted it down, and were on the road again, this time to Sunderland, stopping to briefly look around two large shopping centres on the way.
"What's the clue this time?" Ann asked.
"Start where the train stops, go towards the river bridge, at an island turn west into a street with the name that is wearing well, right, right, into the elevated street, and south from the swimming pool. Making your way to the Queen's wobbly place, keep your eyes open, (Y-Not-U Park) is an option."
"Well, we had better follow the directions," Ann said.
"We could, or we could just start from the swimming pool."
"There could be more than one!"
"Okay, let's follow the clues."
"I wonder what the Queens wobbly place is?"
"Could be a pub," Tony said, and they both chuckled.
"Wasn't that what I said at York?" Ann said.

This was not quite as easy to solve, but they did manage to follow the directions. Although the one way streets had been changed, and some areas pedestrianized, they could not make up their minds if the route was down Low Road,

or the dual carriageway, or Crow Tree Road and Vine Place. But as the centre of the town was small, they walked all the possible routes. Ann noted down absolutely everything they could see between the swimming pool and the place they decided was the Queens wobbly place.
"We'll try to note the rest down later," Tony said.
"Had we better visit each of the car parks, and note what we can see?" Ann asked.
"Y-Not-U Park," Tony said. "Ah... that's a good idea."
They parked in the car park over the Bridges Shopping Centre, and looked around the shops and some exhibitions.

They then headed south. "Is there anywhere else up this way?" Tony asked.
"Yes, Sheffield but we haven't got time."
"We could have, if we used tomorrow. I don't have to be back until five."
"I'm supposed to be working in the morning," Ann said sounding disappointed.
"Time for a car breakdown," Tony said.
"Oh... you are naughty," she laughed.

Tony telephoned the hotel and explained to the Manager that he had a problem with his car.
"Shall I put Ann on a train so she can be back by the morning?" he asked.
"No," the Manager said. "I can cover for her."
"Thanks," said Tony. "See you tomorrow."

They got down to Sheffield and found a place to stay.
"I worked here at one time," Ann told Tony.
"You mean, where we are staying."
"No, in a hotel in the centre."
"So you know your way around?"

"Yes, but there appears to be more one way streets now."
"Well, what's the clue here?" Tony asked.
"Its a counting job; How many car parks are there which are surrounded by the A6134 and A61, assuming the A61 goes from one end of the A6134 to the other along Sheaf Street. Less than 15 - left, 15 - straight on, more than 15 - right."
"Ah, a bit like the sphinx clue at Bentley, can't we do it from a map?" Tony asked.
"Possibly, but it might be a trick question."
"Okay, let's get started."
"Hang on there's a second piece. It says; doing a Sheffield is like going from the City museum, past the University, down Hanover Street and to the Poly."
"Appears on the map to be a sort of U shape, right and right again."

They set about counting the car parks. This was more difficult then they thought it would be due to one way systems and other parts they couldn't drive down. They then went on to the City Museum, on the A57 and followed the route to the Poly, noting the number of roads, directions and anything they thought might be useful.

The following morning, not sure they had found all the car parks they went to find the tourist information centre. They saw a sign near the railway station, and set out to follow it, but the signs took them around in a complete circle. Walking around the circle a second time they spotted the Town Hall, and entering the echo'y entrance hall asked if it was there. Having got directions, they found it.

The girls helping out at the tourist office had no idea how many, they agreed that the ones they had found existed, but could not think of anymore.

A taxi rank was nearby and Tony asked several taxi drivers if they could think of anymore.
"Don't use car parks mate," the first said.
"Just park in the first with a space," the second said looking confused. They could hear him say, "what a wally" as they walked away.

They made their way back, and only just got back by five. Wendy was waiting by the entrance of the hotel.
"You all right?" she asked.
"Yes, why," Tony asked.
"Oh, I was worried, I heard something had happened to your car."

They told her all they had found out, very quickly, as they both had to start work.
"We solved the difficult clue," Ann told her, "the one that said; which town or city was a clock named after, which is known as a Quarter Clock, had dials measuring 8'6," and a bell weighing four tons. It was originally in a town hall. Discover the town or city, and the fall of the weights between windings."
"Oh good," Wendy said.
"Yes," Ann said. "Do you know it has kept perfect time for over 100 years, weighed in total 8 tons, and is one of the largest in the country next to Big Ben on the Houses of Parliament."
"By the way," Wendy said. "That copper, Mickey something, came around looking for one of you, wouldn't say what he wanted but said he would call back tomorrow morning."

CHAPTER TWELVE.

Around 9.30 the next morning there was a knock on the door of Tony's flat.

"Coming," Tony called quickly throwing on a shirt, and putting on some trousers. As he opened the door he could see Mickey Jessett looking cautiously around.

"You on your own?" Mickey asked him.

"Yep."

"Good. I didn't want to bump into your friend."

"Which one?" Tony asked already knowing the answer.

"Ann Croad, I was fairly rude to her last week, and then when I was all muddy, and even one of the police cars went off so I didn't get it dirty, she gave me a lift. I was really embarrassed."

"Bad as each other. You're safe she's working."

"Oh good."

"What can I do for you then?" Tony asked beckoning him in.

"I'm just returning your bicarbonate of soda, it was what you said. I am sure you understand we have a job to do."

"Seemed over keen, especially that dawn entry. Why break the door, why didn't you just knock?"

"If you had been a real dealer," Mickey said uneasily shuffling from one foot to the other and then back again, "You would have got shot of it."

"Oh I see, well thanks for bringing it back. Want some tea?"

"Okay, as long as I don't have to have it in the child's cup." They both laughed, and Tony made some tea and toast.

"You really earn the salary on the statements?" Mickey asked.

"Why officer, I thought you now believed I was innocent," Tony said pretending to be offended.
"No, sorry, I shouldn't have asked."
"Well the answer is yes, but I'll let you into a little secret, there are no children or maintenance payments."
"Don't let Inspector Meldrum know, he hasn't stopped going on about that since. I think he was really jealous."
"Do you get on with him?"
"Well, as well as anyone does. He's very successful, high clear up rate and all that, but me and him don't see eye to eye on our function."
"What do you mean, function?" Tony asked.
"Well in theory, the job of the police is to collect evidence, and if there is enough to warrant a prosecution to hand it over to the Director of Public Prosecutions who decides if they will prosecute."
"So."
"Well, sometimes you either come across evidence that could help the defendant or a witness isn't quite safe, or has forgot, or there are other weaknesses, and well he sometimes sorts of bullies people into saying what he wants."
"He corrupts the course of justice?"
"Well, not exactly, he just helps it along. He sort of bends the rules, he doesn't break them."
"Lucky he didn't plant something here then."
"No he wouldn't do that. Its more the statements he affects."
"How?"
"Well, when we interview somebody initially he tells them what he wants them to say, and then asks them the question. He writes down what he wants to hear, even if it is not what they say. They are then asked to sign his notebook - this is called a 'can say' statement."
"Is that allowed?"
"Well it's justifiable for an arrest, but we have to go back and get a statement signed somewhen."

"So people correct it?"

"Well, not exactly. You see the statements are written up from the 'can say's', and presented to people to read and sign. This is often months, sometimes a year later, most just sign. They can't remember by then if it was him or them that said something."

"But some change them?"

"Well... not exactly, you see he then starts talking about perjury, and charges for wasting police time, and just about everyone is bullied into agreeing."

"But what about when they get to court?"

"Meldrum or the Prosecution gives them a copy of their statement to read, and Meldrum often reinforces the point about perjury, concentrating on it in relation to statements, and they need to say what they had signed."

"But doesn't the defence ask questions?"

"Yes, but by the time people get to court, firstly they are annoyed at having to come, made worse by the long wait, most of which they blame the defendant for, and also they are playing a sort of game, their team is the prosecution. Their main worry is scoring a home goal."

"So the scales of justice don't hang evenly?"

"Well, the judge can often see through it, and corrects it with a suspended sentence."

"I see, Meldrum fixes the evidence, the witnesses lie, the jury find them guilty, and the judge sends the convicted person home."

"Well... yes."

"I'll stay in my kitchen I think."

"I don't blame you, but it's not too bad this week, Meldrum has a week off."

"So you can do your own thing, or did he just pop in to keep up on the progress?"

"No, he's charging all over the country, not like him, he's been to all sorts of places."

"Like the National Pinetum and Bentley Motor Museum."

"Yes, how did you know?"

"Oh. Perhaps I would make a detective."
"Oh well I suppose I had better try and creep out without being seen."

After that he left and that afternoon Tony, Wendy and Ann got together at Tony's suggestion.
"Meldrum has the notebook," Tony said explaining what had been said.
"You're sure it wasn't that Mickey something," Ann said suspiciously. "He could have just been trying to find out what progress we had made."
"Well I didn't tell him anything, and all the places we just visited were on the centre pages so he wouldn't have linked up our trip with the Treasure Hunt," Tony said defensively.
"You're sure he wasn't trying to trick you, they're clever like that," Ann said.
Wendy chuckled, "that's the first time you have suggested the guy is clever."
"What are we going to do?" asked Tony.
"Speed up the search," Ann said.
"We could supply some misleading information," Wendy suggested.
"Okay, let's plan the rest of the search, and Wendy when you have time, see what misleading information we could supply, and Ann you think how we can plant it," Tony said masterfully.
"How about me and Ann going to Poole, and you go to Peterborough tomorrow," Wendy said. "We could all manage that with minimal shift changes, and all be back for five."
"I can fix the rosters okay," Ann said.
"Okay, but we'll have to make an early start," Tony said.
"I can use the zombie," Ann whispered to herself as she left, "to feed false information, so far he has fallen for my tricks."

That evening when Tony and Wendy finished work, they met in Tony's flat for a late snack and a cup of coffee. Ann was still working.

"The other day?" Wendy asked, "last Sunday."

"Yes," Tony replied, not really understanding what she was getting at.

"That lady, um... Monica said I was your latest..... well.... well.... am I?"

"Come here," Tony said and sat her on his lap. "Would you like to be?"

COULD YOU SET UP A LOCAL TREASURE TRAIL CLUB

It's purpose would be:-

To encourage tourism and a better understanding of your area.

To raise money for Charity.

To help people to work together towards the main treasure hunt.

You would:-

Make people's lives more enjoyable.

Help employment in your area.

Help Charities and therefore many people.

Sponsorship is likely to be available locally from hotels and others, including Councils who would like to encourage tourism.

So why not give it a go, either on your own, or get a committee together.

See Appendix Five of this book or write to:-

Federation of Treasure Trail Clubs
c/o Knowledge Base Publications Ltd
19 Penybryn, Mountain Ash
Mid Glamorgan CF45 3TJ.

CHAPTER THIRTEEN

The following morning they were all up early for a 5.30 start and had breakfast together in Tony's flat.
"I didn't know mornings started this early," Tony said rubbing his eyes.
"I haven't been to bed," Wendy said. "I worked through the night on the false clues we can feed. Any ideas Ann on how to get them to them?"
"I realise it will have to be quick, or they will spot. I suggest I call and see the zombie um.... Mickey something and sort of drop a piece of paper. Problem is, he is just daft enough to pick it up and give it back."
"You sure you're not being too hard on him?" Tony said, but wished he hadn't once Ann looked in his direction.
"When?" Tony asked.
"Can't be today, will have to be tomorrow morning. Oh no I had hoped we could do another trip tomorrow."
"I could do it," Wendy said. "He won't be on his guard with me, I can go and see what is happening on the murder. Meldrum won't be there will he...?"
"No, he's away," Tony reassured her.

Soon they were on the road, Ann and Wendy going down to Poole and Tony on his own to Peterborough.

Tony had gone round the dreaded M25 early enough to miss the bad traffic, and took the A1(M) and A1 to Peterborough, picking up a hitch hiker at the Letchworth junction having come off the A1(M) for petrol. He was scruffy, with long hair, looked as if he would be right at home in a hippy commune.

"Going far?" Tony asked.
"Leeds man," replied the man tapping his feet to the music from a personal stereo he was wearing, "and you?"
"Peterborough."
"You live there man?"
"I'm Tony, by the way. No just a.. well sort of business trip."
"A trip that is what I could do with.... I'm Joey, from Leeds. Ain't got any 'ave you?"
"What?" Tony asked suspecting he meant drugs.
"If you got to ask, you ain't got any."
"Okay.... On you're way home?"
"Yep, been to a party. Acid house you know, but the bill raided and I had to dump my stuff."
"You a dealer?"
"No... just sell any spare to pay me way.... you know...."
Tony interrupted, "Had my flat turned over by coppers looking for drugs a couple of weeks ago."
"They find any?"
"No."
"Well done, lucky to have time to dump it."
"I didn't, I didn't have any, and they came in with a sledge hammer early in the morning. They thought they had found something," Tony said starting to laugh, "but it was bicarbonate of soda."
The man sat up, "look like dope does it?"
"White powder, creates a gas, carbon dioxide."
"Would it hurt you if you took some?"
"No, people use it for indigestion."
"Sounds great, where can I get some?"
Why the interest in bicarbonate of soda, Tony wondered, "at any supermarket, with the baking stuff, um... you know flour, spices etc."
"Great. I'll get some."
"What do you want it for?"
"You don't dig the drug scene do you?"
"No."

"Well, you buy an ounce of dope, cut it, that means mix it with a couple of ounces of something else, and you have three ounces to sell."
"That work?"
"Yeah, it's okay as long as you don't kill your customers."
"Not my scene," Tony said thinking help I've picked up a lunatic.
"What you in.... business I mean?"
"I'm a chef in a hotel."
"You cook food.... eh that's good you can get a free meal whenever you like."
Tony laughed, the thought of a hungry chef amused him.
"Not funny man," the hippy said. "It's grub or dope, and I need the dope, but I also have to have some food to stay alive... It's a real waste spending money on food."
"It's a good job not everyone thinks like that, or I would be out of a job."
"I'm a communist, believe in share and share alike, don't see why I should work to let others profit from my labour."
"So you don't claim the dole?"
"Course I do, in four places, but that's a right."
"What! In four places?"
"No, but if I didn't have it the government would only waste it on bombs, nuclear stations and other things."
"What like hospitals," Tony said jokingly.
"No man, they've got you fooled."

Tony had had enough education in this area, and was fed up of the noise of the headphones, which constantly thumped in the background.
"Fancy a coffee?" Tony asked.
"You buying?"
"Yes."
"Okay."
Tony pulled off the road. "How many lifts do you have to get to Leeds?" Tony asked.

"Varies, luckily you're going to Peterborough, that's a long way up."
Tony pulled into a small town called Sandy, and spotted a cafe. "You go on in and grab a table, I'll park the car," Tony said.

But as soon as he could he turned the car round and headed back to the A1. Thank goodness he thought, I'm going to be rid of him.

As he re-entered the A1, there was a girl hitch hiker. At first he was going to drive by, but then he changed his mind. She was obviously very pregnant and as it had just started to rain, was getting wet.

He stopped and opened the passenger door, leaning across the seat. "You're not a drug dealer, communist, or anything are you?" Tony asked.
"No," said the girl looking very surprised.
"Get in then," Tony said. "Sorry, I'm Tony where are you going?"
"Peterborough, and I'm Claire."
"I see you're carrying a passenger, when's it due?"
"In a few weeks."
"Going home?"
"Um... well.... probably."
They chatted away, Tony telling Claire of the treasure trail, Meldrum and the visits he was making, and Claire told him about her sheltered upbringing as the daughter of a minister, and had lived next to her fathers church. She had attended Paddington Tech to do a Medical Technicians course. Claire was 19, had a grandfather who had recently retired, but had been a uniformed police sergeant; and a brother John who had followed her father into the ministry.
"My upbringing was so sheltered," she explained. "We never had booze in the house, so when I went to college I didn't know the effects."

"You didn't know, if you drink, you get drunk."
"Of course, but I thought I could just stop when I'd had enough. I didn't expect it to suddenly affect me."
"And how does drink affect you?"
"Like this," she said pointing to her tummy.
"Oh, I see," Tony said sympathetically.
"No husband, boyfriend.... um baby's father."
"It sounds absolutely terrible, and I only got drunk once, but according to others at the party, I did the rounds so I don't know who's it is."
"So you've given up drinking?"
"I'll never touch another drop."

"Where in Peterborough do you want me to drop you?" Tony asked.
"Anywhere near the centre, I want to look up some old friends," and then "No, I won't, I'll help you solve your clues first."
"Okay," Tony said a little surprised but pleased to have the company. "We are looking for a road that takes you from where you start on a long journey to where you started. Sounds like the M25."
"That's easy," Claire said smiling. "Peterborough has a complete ring road around it."
"It says you start from a place that reminds you of a chair moving."
"Cor, what could that be.... oh how about Castor?"
"You're good at this, aren't you?"
"What next?"
"Past both roads to the crematorium."
"So we go clockwise."
"Cross the Iron Road."
"Railway."
"Turn left to find what David had by 47."
"Let's go and look."
In fact they didn't follow the instructions, but left the A1 at

the Chesterton junction and got onto the ring road up as far as the railway, turning left onto the A15, the road to Lincoln.
"Look out for any mention of David or 47," Tony said.
They had gone just under 2 miles, and round the fourth island.
"All roundabouts here isn't it?" Tony said. "Look there's a 47," and within seconds of turning off had worked out what David had.
"I'll just make a note of it," Tony said. "Not that I would forget."
"Is that it?" Claire said sounding disappointed.
"No we have another riddle about numbers of things this time, it is traffic roundabouts."
"What do we need to know?"
"If there are 40, more or less."
"At a glance I'd say there were a lot more than 40."
"How can we find out?"
"Let's get a street map," Claire suggested, "and count them or.... umm.... if we go back round to Bretton, there's a library where I am sure we can see one."
That is what they did, the riddle said; if there were over 40 to turn left, 40 to go ahead, and less than 40 to turn right. It called this the Peterborough turn.

"Now that's out of the way, where would you like me to take you?" Tony asked Claire.
"Oh... I've changed my mind, I think I'll just go back to London."
"Why!" and it took some coaxing to get Claire to explain that her parents didn't know of her condition, and that she was terrified of telling her father.
"He'll call me all types of names," she said. "He'll never understand."
"Are you sure, how about your grandfather?"
"Um.. yes, but that might cause a family split, I could never

cause that."
"Your brother then?"
"Goodness, he's worse than Dad."
"Fine Christians," Tony said sarcastically.
"Yes, but it's the way of life... sort of... sort of sheltered."
"I see. I have an idea. Has your father preached the story about the good Samaritan?"
"Yes."
"Good, where does he live?"
"I'm not going there," she said looking worried.
"No, I am."
She reluctantly directed him to where her family lived and he parked around the corner.
"Now promise me you will stay here," Tony said.
"Oh, all right, but don't tell him I'm here."
"Okay," and with that Tony put his arm around her and gave her a little hug, "poor thing," he said before getting out and hesitantly approaching the house. I'm not looking forward to this he thought.

Knock, Knock. He could feel his heart beating.
A lady answered.
"Can I see Mr Bateman?"
"Yes, come on in, he's in his study."
Tony was shown into a large, well furnished, well kept house and into the study. Claire's father was deep in some paperwork on his desk.
"What can I do for you?" he asked.
"I... um... sort of wondered if you could give me some advice."
"Well, come and sit down and I will see what I can do."
He didn't seem so bad, Tony thought.
"It's like this," Tony said. "A friend of mine has a problem."
He saw his eyebrows lift, didn't people always start that way when they meant themselves.
"Yes... and what might that be?" he asked.

"Well he was a bit like a good Samaritan, and picked up this girl."

"Oh.. yes," the ministers expression changed. Blimey Tony thought perhaps Claire is right.

"Yes, and she was pregnant."

"Before or after he picked her up, if you know what I mean?"

"Oh, before."

"I see, go on."

"Well, he's sort of trying to help her, you see she's sort of scared to tell her parents, and... and they're devout Christians, and... and I thought you might suggest the best approach."

"Surely if they are devout Christians they would have forgiveness in their hearts for whatever she did."

"She doesn't think so, and... well.... it wasn't her fault."

"A second virgin birth eh," he said sarcastically. Tony was not sure whether to go on, but did, and explained the girl hadn't been used to drink, and had been taken advantage of while under the influence, he thought this sounded better than the way Claire told it.

"I don't see a problem, you just tell your friend to explain that to her parents."

"But she doesn't think they will listen."

"Then you go and explain it to them."

"I just have," Tony whispered.

"Sorry," Claire's father said, "what did you say?"

"I just have, my friend is your daughter Claire."

The ministers neck was getting red, then his face.

"Oh.. I see," he said at last, "and where is Claire now?"

"That depends on how you feel about her," Tony said, hoping he wasn't making the situation worse.

"Well... it was a shock, and I suppose I might have been angry, but you're very clever aren't you? Having told you what a good Christian would do, I'm committed aren't I?"

"Sorry not good enough. Claire deserves more than that, she needs support, understanding and love. Forgiveness just

isn't enough."
"I really think you should let me sort out my relationship with my own daughter."
By this time the lady who had shown him in had come in with some tea and biscuits.
"Did I hear you mention Claire?" she asked. "I'm her mother."
"Oh," Tony said, not wanting to put his foot in it.
The minister explained to his wife exactly what Tony had said, in absolute detail and at the end his wife turned to Tony.
"Are you sure it's Claire, why didn't she come to me, or her grandfather?"
Tony explained that she did not want to split the family.
"I see," said Claire's mother. "So Claire, although having enormous problems is still thinking of us, and setting a far better Christian example than we are."
"Yes," said the minister. "Please ask her to come home, I promise she will have all the love, help and support she needs and no lectures or awkward questions."
"Okay," Tony said getting up and leaving.
"When shall we hear from her?" Claire's mother asked.
"Oh soon," Tony said.

Tony went back to the car and explained what had happened to Claire.
"Will you come in with me?" Claire asked.
"Of course I will."

And that is what he did. There were lots of hugs, and the only tears were in joy at being together again.

Tony didn't stay long, but before he left he gave Claire his address and telephone number and asked her to always

think of him as a friend, if she needed one.
"The best friend anyone could have," she said with tears in her eyes as he drove away.

As Tony drove south on the A1, he felt pleased with himself, but further down he had second thoughts. What if it had all gone terribly wrong he thought. I could have really messed things up for Claire, but by the time he got back to the hotel he was wondering how Ann and Wendy were getting on, and thought back to the morning when they had all left.

They had, as you will recall, all had breakfast together before Ann and Wendy set off in Ann's car.
"Poole here we come," Ann said.
"Oh, the life on the ocean waves," Wendy sang.
"Are you interested in boats, Wendy?"
"No, can't swim, but I could get interested if we met a millionaire with a luxury yacht."
"And I thought you were interested in Tony."
"Yes, but he doesn't seem interested in me."
"I wouldn't say that, he's just... well... nice."
"You're dead keen on him, aren't you?"
"Maybe, but he's my friend. I want him to be happy, and well if I'm not the girl he wants, then well, I just want him to be happy."
"You don't think you could make him happy?"
"Yes, well I would hope so."
"Ann, you are normally so confident about everything, I mean think how you handled the police, and run the hotel."
"Yes, but that's different. Tony is special, and I just.... well just want him to be happy."
They both thought quietly as they drove along. Ann, of how much she would like to marry Tony, and Wendy of how much Ann was in love with Tony, even if she wouldn't

admit it.

Wendy made a decision, she would not get in Ann's way, after all Ann was her friend, and yes, she liked Tony as well but, she told herself there were many more men, she was young, and there was plenty of time.

Perhaps, she thought, I can help Ann do a makeover, change her hairstyle, clothes, make her look a bit more.. well.... sexy.
"Ann I have an idea, why don't we swap ideas on dressing and making up, you give me a makeover, and I will do the same for you."
"Shopping," Ann said and then hesitantly. "You're not tactfully telling me I'm scruffy are you?" Ann asked.
"No, of course not, just a bit of fun, and think how Tony would be surprised to see you in a short skirt, or slinky trousers, and me in sensible clothes for a change."
"Okay... we'll do it."

Their trip to Poole proved to be an exciting day. They visited Cobbs Quay, a marina and yacht club, and looked at boats for sale. They even had a test drive in a 32ft sports cruiser. They then drove around to Sandbanks and got the ferry to Brownsea Island.
"What are we doing here?" Ann asked. "We know the treasure is on the mainland."
"A clue says Brownsea Island is a point of departure," Wendy said, "but the only point you can go back to is Sandbanks."
"Is that it?" Ann asked.
"No, it says like Green Island, Furzey Island, Brownsea Island, West Lake and the Blue Lagoon are."
"What is?" Ann asked.

"It doesn't say."

They got a ferry trip around the harbour from Poole Quay and asked a lot of questions, saw each of the islands from a boat, and found the Blue Lagoon, but as by this time the tide was out it would have been better called the Mud Hole.

"They all have piers or landing strips," Ann said. "All the islands and the Blue Lagoon."
"Yes, but so does everything else around here. There are so many boats around here, that I even saw one place lifting the boats out with a sort of fork lift truck, and storing them on a sort of car park."
"Okay, let's make lots of notes, and make sense of it somewhen else," Ann suggested.
And that is what they did, before getting a bit of shopping in on the way back.

On the way back they plotted a surprise for Tony.
Ann chuckled, "I bet he'll be speechless."

CHAPTER FOURTEEN.

A couple of days later, the girls were ready to spring their surprise on Tony.

Although he had told them about the clues, and two hitch hikers, he hadn't mentioned Claire's condition, or the meeting with her family. Well that would be too much like showing off. He just said that a student he picked up had helped him solve the clues, and the girls said that perhaps they should have picked up some hitch hikers as well to help them.

Tony had a lay in, and was just getting up at 10.30, well it was more than just a bit of a lay in, and he was supposed to start work at eleven, when Wendy arrived, dressed in trousers, jumper, and having her hair up in a sort of cap.
"I was only joking about decorating my flat," Tony said, noticing her lack of glamour.
"Don't you like my new look?" she asked him.
"Well... well..." how could he say it without hurting her feelings, "it looks very practical."
"But do you like it?" she pressed.
"Well.... well.... I'll probably get used to it, but I always like the way you look," phew, he thought, I got away with it.
At that moment Ann arrived, dressed in the shortest mini-skirt he had seen, with net stockings, a thin shaped blouse that showed off quite a surprisingly good figure, and a pony tail.
"How did you do that, grow your hair so fast?" Tony asked.
"It's a hair piece, looks real doesn't it?" she said trying to look as sexy as possible.

"Well... well.... I'm.... I'm...."

"Speechless?" Wendy asked.

"Yes, speechless."

He couldn't help staring at Ann, but tried not to, "are you going somewhere special?" he asked her.

"No. It's just Wendy said she was going to have a new image, and I thought I might as well too."

"You mean you're going to dress like that all the time," Tony asked in surprise.

"Why don't you like it?"

"Yes, but it's hardly practical for working in the hotel."

"Sorry," she said pretending to be angry. "But I never heard you tell Wendy that when she dressed up nice."

Tony didn't know what to say, or where to look. How could he explain to Ann without upsetting her, or upsetting Wendy.

"Well," Wendy said. "Don't you like girls to dress like that, didn't you like the old me?"

How could he explain, he liked them as they were, sensible, chuckly, happy, reliable Ann, and well Wendy was clever, but well, he liked her to look sexy as well. He was really embarrassed, he didn't know what to say.

Suddenly the girls broke out in a giggle, "don't look so worried," Ann said, "we're just playing a trick on you."

"Oh," he said relieved. "But what is the answer, why do I prefer you both as you were?"

"I suppose you just consider the way we dress part of our personalities," Wendy said thoughtfully, "but you must agree Ann looks really good doesn't she?"

"Yes, but it's not really Ann is it?"

"You mean you wouldn't want to go out with me like this?" Ann said hitching her short skirt up another two inches.

"Would you want to go out with me, if I left my trousers at home?" Tony asked and when he didn't receive an answer; "I would be frightened to put my arm round you like that in

case something popped out of your blouse."
They laughed so much that everything nearly did pop out.

The following day, Wendy was working, but Tony and Ann managed to get away on another trip. Ann had offered to re-schedule Wendy so she could go too, but Wendy had made a excuse about a dentist appointment. In fact there was no dentist appointment, she just wanted to give Ann and Tony some time together.

They took Ann's car, although Tony drove to start. First stop Oxford. Around the M25, up the M40. "Another town with a ring road," Tony said. "Not more roundabouts to count, I hope."
"No, it says; from Blenheim to Blenheim Palace, as the crow flies, pass over the services, at which point the aircraft taking off frightened the crow, making it fly in the opposite direction. Just before it saw some unusual plants, it spotted something else that reminded it of walking trees."
"Blimey," Tony said. "What's in Oxford" then, "isn't Blenheim Palace at Woodstock?"
"Yes, but Blenheim is sort of East of Oxford, and if you draw a line between the two you cross the services on the ring road. It's where the A44 crosses the A34."
"Are there services there?"
"Yes, and to the north north west is Oxford Airport."
"So where did the crow go?" Tony asked.
"Well it says in the opposite direction, so just to the east of the City Centre."
"What is there that could have unusual plants, or remind the crow of walking trees?"
"That's what were going to find out, but unusual plants could be some sort of obscure reference to students or something, with all the colleges there."
"Really," Tony said in surprise. "Are they on the line you

think the crow would fly?"
"Well about three are, Lady Margaret Hall, Manchester and St Catherine's. Most of the others would be too far to the west."
"How about walking trees?" Tony asked.
"Several bits of river are in the right place, could be tress on an island, with moving water flowing by, to create the impression of the trees moving."

They went into Oxford, and visited each of the sites in turn, ending up at Manchester College, established in 1818. "Look," Tony said "across the road."
"Oh. That could be it," Ann said.
"Now what about the walking trees?"
"Ask some students," Ann suggested.
They did, but did not get any helpful suggestions.
"There's a recreation ground," Ann said, "let's look in there."
"Okay, but we'd better be quick, there are several other places to go today."

In fact it didn't take them long to work out what it was, and they were soon on their way. This time to Northampton.

"What now?" Tony asked, "Northampton is not far now."
"It says; south of the services, west of the motorway, east of the horses, and north of hills of bricks lies a town not far from Northampton."
"Stop a moment, we need to work that one out with a map."
"I have it, I think its Milton Keynes."
"Okay," Tony said, "but do we have anything else in Northampton?"
"Yes, its another left, right puzzle."
"If Northampton has 8 or more churches it equals left. If

not it goes right."
"Okay, so where do we start, how about finding a library, they might be able to help."
"Good idea," Ann said.

This is what they did, and solved the puzzle without much difficulty, before going back down to Milton Keynes. Tony had done all the driving so far and was starting to get tired.
"You reckon the other place near Northampton is Milton Keynes? It's not very near. I wouldn't want to walk it," Tony said with some concern that they were in the wrong place.
"It says it's a modern town," Ann reassured him, "and Milton Keynes is."
"What are we looking for, not more counting?"
"It says; find the lake that looks like a premature creature and follow a main road west across many islands. You are on the way to the port, over the largest island, and turn left. Keep going to see something that could be fun."
"Well we can follow that," Tony said. "I can see the lake on the map, and the road is the main A509, I think."
"Okay, and the biggest island will presumably be in the city centre," Ann added.

They drove along for some time, twice getting lost due to the vast number of traffic islands. Eventually they found it although they nearly missed it as neither were involved in the hobby, or should I call it a sport.

"Where next?" Tony asked, already feeling quite tired.
"Cambridge," Ann said.
"Isn't that too far for today?" Tony asked hoping she would say yes.
"No, we can manage Cambridge."

Tony gave a big sigh, "Are you sure?"
"Yes, I can drive for a bit," and they swapped over.

From Milton Keynes they went through Bedford, and St Neots arriving at Cambridge.
"What is it this time?" Tony asked.
"I don't know, you've got the sheet there," Ann said pointing to the glove box.
"Oh, yes, it says; Cambridge like Oxford has many colleges and a full ring. It has however something else in common, far older than education, or even people."
"Must be something to do with the landscape or an old forest or something."
"I didn't notice a forest in Oxford," Tony said.
"How about an earthworks, or chapel, or something."
"That wouldn't be older than people."
"Perhaps its the type of stone, or soil."

They visited museums, a library, and looked at local maps, but what could be older than people?

They were on their way from the shopping centre to the folk museum, when Ann said "Oh, how stupid, of course, how could we not see it before?"
Tony, of course, still hadn't seen it, and just stood looking around in all directions.
"Think," she said pointing down, "there," waving her hand into the distance.
"Of course," Tony said.

They left Cambridge not knowing that the answer to another clue would again point to Cambridge, but that's another story.

As they drove back, Ann turned to Tony, "Are you sitting comfortably? Yes, then I'll begin." She told him what good friends they were, and how much fun they had, and reminded him of all the best moments. This is what she had been building up to, she hesitated, not daring to look around. "I love you," she said, "I want us to be more than just friends, maybe get married when you are ready." There was no reply.

Oh, well at least he didn't say no, perhaps he was speechless, she continued, "perhaps start a family, perhaps start practising tonight," was that going too far, she hesitated. Still no reply. "What do you think?"
Still no reply, perhaps he was lost for words, or perhaps he didn't know how to say no. Oh, what had she done, was she spoiling a wonderful friendship?
"Please say no if you want," she said. "I... I won't be offended." Still no reply. She waited, and eventually couldn't wait any longer. Looking around slowly, she let out a sigh of relief. Goodness he must have been tired, she thought he's gone fast asleep.

A little while later he woke up.
"Sorry," he said. "How rude of me to go to sleep while you were talking.
"Oh, that's okay," she said relieved she hadn't messed everything up.
"I'm awake now, so please tell me again."
"I was just saying how much I enjoy your company and I hope we can always be friends."
"Can't see why not," he replied. "After all, you're my very best friend, aren't you?"

A little further on Tony said, "Will we get back again tonight, or do you want to spend the night in a motel?"

Had he heard what she had said, "up to you," she said as her heart lost a beat or two.

CHAPTER FIFTEEN.

A couple of days later Wendy came around to Tony's flat to borrow some toilet paper. What a thing to run out of, she thought. She had her cotton mini nightdress on, and had just thrown a coat over her shoulder.

She knocked, but there was no reply. He said let myself in, she thought. So still having a key she let herself in quietly so not to wake him.

Tony must still be asleep she thought, and dropping her coat on the chair went into the bathroom, where there was a cupboard that spare toilet rolls were kept.

She was concentrating so much on being quiet, and listening for any noise from the bedroom, that she was totally inside the bathroom before she realised Tony was stood in front of her with just a towel wrapped around him.
"Sorry," she said. "I thought you were still asleep. I just wanted to borrow a loo roll," but as she reached past him towards the cupboard she knocked off his towel, and in his mad attempt to grab it, he knocked her off balance. Splash, Tony ended up in the bath, with Wendy on top of him. I don't know who was most embarrassed, Tony because he didn't have anything on, or Wendy because when her nightdress got wet it went transparent.
"Sorry," Tony said. "I just lost my balance."
Seeing the funny side of it Wendy said, "now who is molesting who," and they both laughed, which of course relieved all their embarrassment.
"What do we do now?" Wendy asked. "I can't go back looking like this."
"So why not relax and have a soak," Tony joked, "but

there's only one problem I have cramp in my leg."
"Here let me rub it for you," and then she tried to get out only slipping back, this time facing him.
"Oopps," Wendy said.
"I'm not complaining," Tony said. "But if we are staying we had better put some more hot water in."
She was just about to suggest another way to keep warm when she remembered Ann, and her decision not to come between them.
"Quick," she said "help me up. I have just remembered I left something on my stove," and within a second or two had managed to get out of the bath, and gathered her coat and went.

"Drat," Tony said to himself. "I shouldn't have embarrassed her like that," looking at himself in the mirror. He felt a little disappointed, but he wasn't quite sure if it was in his actions, or that she had left, at that moment.

Wendy on the other hand was sitting in her flat thinking. Could she go through with this idea of getting Tony and Ann together when all she really wanted was to be with him. No, she said to herself, I won't be just a plaything, let Ann have a chance first. But then she thought it wouldn't hurt to tease him just a little.

So putting on a low cut blouse, and with a small skirt she went back around to apologise of course, although she didn't knock, but just let herself in with her key.

"Please think nothing of it," Tony said. "After all nothing really terrible happened." The clothes, or lack of them, had the desired effect, and Tony had great difficulty keeping his hands off her.

More to get his mind off Wendy than anything else, he suggested they tackle some more puzzles in the notebook.
"This one," Tony said, "I think points to Peterborough." It was a clue relating to places various families came from, and he had found each had ancestors from Peterborough when looking them up, in the green brick."
"That's good," Wendy said. "I think we can also use the brick to solve the longest one, that's written in some sort of code."
"How?"
"Well, I remember reading somewhere that you can add up the number of each letter, and get the distribution of the letters. So if the most common letter is 'E' then the most common letter in the coded piece can be turned into an 'E', and so on."
"So we add up all the letters, I mean the number that is used in the book, and in the coded piece, and super impose one for the other depending on the occurrence."
"Yep," said Wendy feeling pleased with herself.
"Okay, but why use the brick?"
"Well," explained Wendy. "The author of the brick is a person who grew up in England and moved to Wales. Within a few miles of the author of the brick John Pugh lived, who had also moved from England, so their pattern or words would be similar."
"You're a genius," Tony said.
"Not just a blonde bimbo anymore," she said smiling.

They got started at once. Wendy analysing the article from the book, "Um yes, the Getting Started article will do," and Tony analysing the coded piece of text. This, you will

THE EXACT LOCATION

This coded section will allow you, with a little research and thought to find and have my treasure. Of course you have to break the code first, but I haven't made it too difficult.

WHCCF, DHCSFVH. MHZ MFX JBH J AHRLXZ JRN ZWFXCN EH TCHJZHN DLIW MFXB TBFDHBZ FU SFNH EBHJYLRA. L JV JEFXI IF IHCC MFX IWH HQJSI CFSJILFR FU IWH SFRIJLRHB, DWLSW DLCC ALKH MFX ULRJC LRZIBXSILFRZ IF AHI IWH IBHJZXBH. IWH ULRJC LRZIBXSILFRZ JBH DBLIIHR LR IWH ZJVH SFNH JZ IWLZ TJAH, JRN RFD MFX YRFD LI, MFX DLCC EH JECH IF AHI MFXB WJRNZ FR IWH VFRHM. IWH ULRJC LRZIBXSILFRZ JBH IWH TJZZDFBN FB SFNH JRN NHIJLCZ FR DWF, FB WFD IF XZH LI. LI LZ HOXLKJCHRI IF J UXCC IBHJZXBH SWHZI. IWH SFRIJLRHB IWHZH LRZIBXSILFRZ JBH LR DHLAWZ JEFXI ZHKHRIHHR TFXRNZ, IWJI'Z JEFXI IWH ZJVH JZ HLAWI EJAZ FU ZXAJB. LI LZR'I EXBLHN, JRN SJR EH ZHHR UBFV IWH TCJSH IWHZH LRZIBXSILFRZ DLCC IJYH MFX.

IWH UFCCFDLRA LRZIBXSILFRZ IJYHZ MFX IWH CJZI ULKH JRN WJCU VLCHZ. MFX SJR NHNXSH UBFV FIWHB SCXHZ LR IWH RFIHEFFY DWHBH MFX ZIJBI IWLZ ZFCXILFR. L DLCC IHCC MFX LI LZ FR J VJLR BFJN. LU IBJKHCCLRA EM SJB MFX SJR AHI HJZLCM DLIWLR FRH WXRNBHN MJBNZ, EXI MFX DLCC RHHN IF NF IWH CJZI TJBI FR UFFI.

appreciate, took some time but Tony having the shorter text finished first, and was just sitting looking at the lovely thing opposite, when there was a knock on the door.

Answering it, he found both Ann and Mickey Jessett there.
"Need an umpire," Tony said, being surprised to see them together.
"No, we just both happened to be coming this way," Ann said getting through the door first.
Turning to Mickey, Tony said "well what brings you here again?" not being sure if he was really pleased to see him.
"Come on in anyway," Tony continued.
"It's a bit awkward," Mickey said. "Do you know a man called John Stroud, sometimes known as Joey."
"No..." Tony said thoughtfully. "I don't think I do... why?"
"Well someone said they saw you drop him at a cafe, well actually they had your car number."
"Sorry, it doesn't ring a bell," Tony said. "Tell me more about him."
"Well this is where it is awkward. I'm not suggesting anything you see, but he is a known drug dealer, and we found his body, and he had several containers of bicarbonate of soda in his pockets."
"Ah...," Tony said. "The hippy..... body did you say."
"Yes, he's dead, so you did know him?"
Tony explained about the hitch hiker, conversation, and depositing him, together with the discussion about cutting drugs."
"Well I appreciate your frankness, but it's a pity you couldn't have reported it."
"Why would it have made any difference?"
"In this case, no."
"Miss Lewis," Mickey said turning to Wendy. "We need somewhen to get a better statement from you."
"I suffer from amnesia," Wendy said. "I can hardly remember my own name, so you know everything I can tell you."

The Exact Location contd...

DJIHBTBFFU UFFIDJBH VLAWI EH XZHUXC.

MFX DLCC RFI WJKH IF AF JRMDWHBH MFX NF RFI WJKH UBHH JSSHZZ, NF JRM NJVJAH, FB NLA JRM WFCHZ. IWH SFRIJLRHB EHLRA FR FTHR NLZTCJM.

L WJKH JNNHN J UHD TXGGCHZ, LR WHBH PXZI IF VJYH MFX IWLRY J CLIICH.

AFFN CXSY JRN NBLKH SJBHUXCCM.

AFLRA LR IWH NLBHSILFR FU IWH BHUHBHRSH TFLRI, TBFSHHN XRILC MFX AHI IF J TFLRI IWJI VJYHZ MFX IWLRY FU HCHSIBLSLIM, JRN JTTHJBZ IF HUUHSI VM TJSHVJYHB. NF J ZWHUULHCN JRN GHBF. TBFSHHN XRILC MFX ZHH DWJI NJKLN WJN FR MFXB EBLZIFC ZLNH, JRN IXBR. MFX DLCC EH BHVLRNHN FU ZFVHDWHBH MFX DLCC WJKH EHHR. WJKLRA IBJKHCCHN WJCU J VLCH MFX JBH CHJKLRA IWH ZVJCC NFRYHM EHWLRN, JI ZHKHR IHRIWZ MFX SBFZZ J EBLNAH JRN JI J VLCH TJZZ J BFJN IWJI NFHZ RFI AF JRMDWHBH. EM FRH JRN J WJCU VLCHZ MFX JBH JVFRAZI IWH IBHZZ, JRN BHVLRNHN FU IWH TLRHIXV, DWHR MFX IXBR LR IWH EHRICHM NLBHSILFR. IDF VLCHZ JRN MFX TJZZ J UFFITJIW FR MFXB BLAWI IWJI JTTHJBZ IF AF XT J DJCC.

ZIFT J VFVHRI WHBH, LU MFX JBH J TWFIFABJTWHB NF MFXB ZIXUU, LU JR

"That's not very helpful."
"Well after last time, what do you expect?"
"Oh. I see, you're still annoyed about that."
Ann interrupted at this point, "hardly surprising is it after you and that guy suggested she had an affair with her boss and then murdered him. You even suggested she threatened him."
"Oh. I see. It isn't personal; just doing my job."
"Well, why can't you do it pleasantly," Ann snapped back at him.
"Ding, ding," Tony said "end of round one."
Mickey Jessett took this opportunity to say goodbye and got out.
"The nerve of that guy," Ann said.

They explained to Ann, how they planned to break the coded clue, and after a little while they had all the counts they needed to do the decoding.
"Now let's start with the most common letter, 'E', what is the most common letter in the coded piece."
Tony told her, and Tony replaced all of them with 'E's, and did the same for each letter.
"Now let's write it out again," Wendy said, "and see what we have."
"Doesn't look like words," Ann said disappointedly.
"Oh," Wendy said. "I was hoping it would be nearer than that. I know single words have to be I or A, and double letter words can only be AN, IF, IS, TO, and a few others."

By this means they discovered that, A was correct, I and N had been swapped, as had O and T, R and S, and P and B. They discovered that E, A, H, V, K, and X had come out correctly, and the other groups were often just swapped slightly, or with a larger group, most of the letters had slipped by one position.
"That's it," Ann said. "It starts Hello Welcome."

The Exact Location contd...

JBILZI, BHVHVEHB IWH ZSHRH JWHJN UFB UXIXBH LRZTLBJILFR.

IDF TFLRI RLRH VLCHZ JRN MFX SBFZZ IDF EBLNAHZ. SFRILRXLRA JEFXI J IHRIW FU J VLCH JUIHB IWH TFZIEFQ, IXBR LR IWH HQHIHB NLBHSILFR.

JI IWBHH TFLRI IWBHH VLCHZ, TJZZ, CHJKLRA LI JZ LI DJZ. UFXB VLCHZ, JRN MFX JBH FR J AFFN BFJN.

JI UFXB JRN IWBHH OXJBIHBZ, IWHBH AFHZ VM TJSHVJYHB JAJLR, JW... HCHSIBLSLIM L IWLRY.

MFX VJM ZHH J DJCCHN AJBNHR RFD, EXI L EHI MFX SJR'I ZHH IWH WFXZH.

RFD FR MFXB EHRICHM ZLNH, MFX ZHH DWJI FQUFBN JRN SJVEBLNAH WJN. NFR'I DFBBM LI SFVHZ IF MFX JI IWH ECLRN TJBI.

TJZI IWH VLRL CJRNZCLNH, MFX ZHH IDF FU IWH IWLRAZ. IWH IWLRAZ VLAWI EHCFRA IF WHB, FB EH SFSYRHM AFCN.

CFFY JBFXRN, RF FRH, RF WFXZH, RFIWLRA SJR ZHH MFX. IWHBH LZ RF TBFTHBIM, RFIWLRA FU KJCXH, FIWHB IWJR IWH BFJN

IWHBH LZ CLIICH WHBH IWJI DFXCN RFI WJKH EHHR WHBH DWHR NLRFZJXBZ BFJVHN

At that point Tony interrupted her "yes, but look, down here, it gives exact directions, and look it says;" he said reading it out word for word "and the container is now in sight. It is waiting for you, no shovel or digging."
"And here," Wendy said excitedly, "the container weighs about seventeen pounds, how big is that?"
"Goodness," Ann said. "That would depend what it was made of, if it was metal I would guess the size of a suitcase, but of wood, it could be bigger."
"But....," Tony said. "But how can it be..... look it says here again it isn't buried, so why don't other people find it."
"It says it's camouflaged," Wendy pointed out, "so maybe it looks like a log, lying on the floor in a forest or something."

They spent some time reading and re-reading the instructions, which covered a distance of at least five and a half miles, and gave details of bridges, road junctions and much more.

"No wonder it kept saying keep your eyes open, with this much detail, we could probably spot it, without solving all the rest of the clues," Tony said.
"You need them to use in this," Wendy pointed out, "but I agree it is very detailed."
"Have we got enough detail to solve it on a map ?," Ann asked.
"Um, possibly, power lines, two bridges, possibly road and railway, or railway and canal, wood or forest, it's worth a go," Tony said looking for volunteers.
"Okay," Ann said masterfully. "I will get some detailed maps of the areas we have visited."

"Fantastic, we are a lot nearer now," Tony said, "but did the copper see what we were doing?"

The Exact Location contd...

IWH HJBIW.

UBFV IWHV IWLRAZ.

VFKH FR J VJARHILS EHJBLRA FU JRZDHB LR BHCJILFR IF IWH BHUHBHRSH TFLRI.

IJYH NBLKLRA CLSHRSH NJIH JRN NLKLNH EM IWH RXVEHB FU ZTWLRQHZ, JRN BFXRN IF RHJBHZI RXVEHB. JNN IWH RXVEHB FU THFTCH IF ZHH FKHB IWH FCN VJR FU YHRI, JRN IWH RXVEHB FU FSIJAFRZ, JRN ZXEIBJSI IWH RXVEHB FU ZTWLRQHZ (JZ IWHM DFXCN EH FXI FU TCJSH WHBH), JRN DH WJKH IWH JRZDHB. MFX JBH LU MFX WJKH VJRJAHN IWLZ SFBBHSICM, DJCYLRA RFI UJB UBFV IWH RHD NLBHSILFR.

IBJKHC FRH UFFI UFB HKHBM ELBN TJLRILRA, JRN IWH SFRIJLRHB LZ RFD LR ZLAWI. LI LZ DJLILRA UFB MFX, RF ZWFKHC, FB NLAALRA, LI ZLIZ IWHLB DJLILRA UFB MFX IF IJYH MFXB IBHJZXBH. IWH SFRIJLRHB DHLAWZ ZHKHRIHHR TFXRNZ FB IWHBH JEFXIZ, JRN VJM EH PXZI J CLIICH SJVFXUCJAHN.

LU MFX NFR'I ZHH LI JI FRSH, IWHR YHHT IWH CFSJILFR ZHSBHI JRN SFVH EJSY JRFIWHB NJM, JRN CHI MFXB HMHZ HRCLAWIHR MFX. TCHJZH BHVHVEHB RF NLAALRA FB NJVJAH RHHNZ IF EH NFRH.

"No. I don't think so," Wendy said confidently. "I covered up all my workings while he was here, and you had already finished your analysis."

"You will never guess what happened this morning," Wendy said looking at Tony, and smiling.

"What?" asked Ann.

And Tony interrupted, "we decided one of the other puzzles pointed to Peterborough."

"That's what I was going to say," Wendy said. And thought, and everything else that happened this morning is a secret.

BREAKING CODES

The simplest way of breaking simple codes is by counting the numbers of each character in the coded and standard text. This will work for this example. To do this:-

1. Add up the number of each letter in the coded text.
2. Add up the number of each letter in a piece of chosen normal text.
3. Put both lists in order by the number of times a letter has occurred, so the most popular one (E) is at the top.
4. Make up a provisional decode list, by writing the most common letter of each list together. So you have pairs of letters down the page.
5. Use the decode list to convert the coded text into a provisionally decoded text.
6. Next apply logic. Single letters have to be I or A, there are very few words with two or three letters.
7. Letters you have decoded in Step 6 can be corrected on the decode list. Usually they will only be one step out. This will allow you to correct the decode list.
8. Use the corrected decode list to get a final decoded text.
9. Keep the final decode list. You will need it again.
10. Keep the solution to yourself. After all you have done the work.

TIP: The text of this chapter tells you some of the changes between the provisional decode list and final decode list, which would allow you to get a more accurate provisional decode list to use in step six.

CHAPTER SIXTEEN.

A few days later, on Saturday morning, Tony and Ann were studying maps in Tony's flat.
"I can't see where this could be," Tony said in frustration.
"How about drawing a sketch map of the instructions, and see if that helps?" Ann suggested.
"We don't know all the clues," Tony said, looking in detail at the decoded text.
"Okay, what do we need?"
"Oh, not much, mainly the clues at Bristol and Exeter."
"Okay," Ann said, "I can reschedule Wendy so we can all go Monday."
"Great!"

Wendy was working this Saturday morning, and had just helped one of the guests, that she didn't like much. As he walked away she counted her fingers to make sure they were all still there. Mr Oliver Robson, she thought, I wonder what you do. There were numerous rumours, some linking him with the secret service, and definitely in his room, according to the hotel staff, Wendy had heard of the elaborate audio and video equipment. There was something about him, that made him seem a shady character. Perhaps it was his manner, or the fact that he was always a loner.

"Lost a finger?" the man in front of her said, making her jump.
"Sorry!" Wendy said.
"The Merryweather family booking in."
"Ah, yes Mr Merryweather," and Wendy looked up their booking and started to book them in, when she became

aware that his wife appeared disturbed at something.
"Problem?" Wendy said.
"Um.. No," said the lady seeming a little embarrassed.
"Shall I book a table for lunch or dinner?" Wendy asked.
"I'd love to," Mr Merryweather said, "but we have a special needs child, he's not too easy to control, and tends to make a mess, so I think we had better find a cafe or something."
Wendy looked over the counter to see a little boy, with a big beaming smile. "This one?" Wendy asked, as there were three others behind. She guessed the boy would be about five, his sister nine or ten and the other two around sixteen or seventeen.
"Yes," said the man patting the boy on the head.
"Okay, um... Wait a moment I will see what I can arrange," Wendy said wondering what to do next, and reaching for the intercom.
"Hello, can I speak to Ann?"
She had spoken to Tony, who put Ann on.
"Hi, can you help Ann?" and she explained the situation to her.
"We're coming over," Ann said.
Wendy explained to the customers who she had called and within a few minutes Ann and Tony arrived.
"No problem," Ann said. "I can get you a booth, and use disposable tablecloths, so there will be no problem."
And at that moment Ann felt a hand going up her skirt, which at first she ignored thinking it was Tony fooling about, but when it got higher she jumped, and looking around found the boy with the big smile.
"Tickle, tickle," he said.
His parents explained that although he didn't talk, he could say just a few words, and made friends with people by giving them a tickle.
"Tickle... tickle," Tony said giving the little boy a tickle, and getting a screech of excitement.
Tony spent sometime talking to the family. They discussed the children, their trip, Mr Merryweather's job with

computers and the place they came from, a little place called Honeybourne, which Tony soon discovered was the same place as Cow Honeybourne that was mentioned in the notebook, and where he thought his distant relative had come from before moving to Wales.

After the Merryweather's had booked in, and were shown to their rooms, they came back down and talked to Ann and Tony in the bar. By this time, Billy the smiling boy, and Tony were the best of friends.

When Wendy came over to them to tell them their table was now ready, she pointed out Oliver Robson, further down the bar to Tony.
"Look, he signed in as Oliver Robson, but he has KM on his shirt cuffs," Wendy said.
"Down on his luck," Mrs Merryweather suggested, "secondhand shirts."

Perhaps noticing them looking at him, Oliver Robson came over.
"Hi, Oliver Robson.... I'm in antiques. Did I hear you say you were from Honeybourne?"
"Yes," just about all the Merryweather's said at once.
"Know it well.... often at Broadway.... antiques you know."
As their table was ready, and no one else was interested in antiques, the conversation soon fizzled out, and as they went to their table Tony volunteered to look after Billy for a while in the afternoon to give the rest of them some time on their own. Mrs Merryweather was at first reluctant, but her husband reassured her, and Billy would have been happy to have gone off at that time, if he hadn't spotted the dining tables ahead.

As arranged that afternoon Tony looked after Billy, and it

was an uneventful afternoon except for one point when Tony and Billy were playing a tickling game on the bed, and Tony thought he heard someone in the other room, but no one was there.

Later that evening while looking at the map Tony spotted a place he thought matched up with the decoded instructions. "I'll go and check this out," Tony said "and you girls go and explore Bristol and Exeter."

The next morning Tony got a message from Wendy on reception. She didn't sound too pleased.
"Hi, Mr Hyatt I have a message for you," she said in an annoyed sort of voice.
"Anything the matter?" Tony asked.
"No," Wendy snapped. "The message is that Claire has had the baby, she and baby are doing well, it's a boy and they are naming it after you."
"Oh, that's nice", Tony said, but heard the other end of the intercom disconnect in the middle.
She must have got out of the wrong side of the bed this morning, he thought.

A little later both Wendy and Ann came across and questioned him about who Claire was, and exactly what his relationship was with her.

What did they think of him, he wondered, but he soon spotted that Ann was teasing him. Although he wasn't so sure about Wendy, who was cool towards him the rest of the day.

Tony set off early the next morning, relieved to get away on his own. Away from that suspicious Wendy. Why didn't she have a better opinion of him, he wondered.

The two girls set off in Ann's car, but had just gone a few yards down the road, when it cut out, and they couldn't get it going again.

Wendy offered to use her car, but Ann insisted they hire one. So around an hour later they eventually set out.

At Bristol, they had a quick look around, and turned up a hill that had lots of book shops.
"Reminds me of York," Ann said, but couldn't think why.

They found Clifton, and the famous Suspension Bridge designed by Brunel, and then near to it was the camera obscurer. They didn't have to queue long to see it, and they went down a tunnel in the ground coming out on the cliff face.
"All we need to know," Ann said, "is which way to the Suspension Bridge."
"Back up the steps," Wendy said not liking the cave like nature of the tunnel.
Looking out of the opening on a balcony along way up, they quickly wrote down the answer before leaving and going back into Bristol to find the SS Great Britain, a massive old ship being restored. The notebook just said it would be worth a visit, and it was. They learnt all about it and made a lot of notes, before going on under the Suspension Bridge to the M5 and on down to Exeter.

They looked around Exeter, and its shops, saw what is said to be the narrowest street in Britain, and then went to the Cathedral.
"What is the clue?" Wendy asked.

"It say's; a crow flew from the Cathedral to library, prison and landed on the fire station tower. After a rest he flew due east until he got to the railway line, then due south to the river, and back to the Cathedral. As he always flew quite high, he used a ruined chapel as a reference point which side was it on, left or right. The crow eventually decided on his holidays, and flies to a tropical sounding place you have seen."
"Where shall we start?"
"I tried to look at a map, but not all the places are mentioned. So I suggest we find them all and work out where he would have flown, and look for a common point."
"What about the tropical place?" Wendy asked.
"It's not part of this puzzle, it could be part of what is called the alternative something, but so far we have ignored that."

They asked various people where the points mentioned were, and drove around, before deciding if it was left or right.

They set off back up the M5, and along the M4, stopping for something to drink at the Leigh Delamere services near Chippenham. They had talked over all the clues, discussed Tony, the hotel and many other topics, and were in the middle of a chuckle about not standing under pigeons or crows, as they went past the Swindon exit junction 16, when Ann suddenly stood on the brakes. A lorry was out of control and coming down off the roundabout above, down the grass bank, and across the carriageway.
"Fast reaction," Wendy said as they stopped a few feet short of the upturned lorry that had now come to rest across the carriageway.
"Oh, no," Ann said looking in her mirror and seeing a coach approaching at full speed behind.
Wendy did not even have time to look around before there was a sound of twisting metal and their car was squeezed

between the coach and the upturned lorry.

Ann was trapped when she came round, there was lots of noise, she could see people, but was totally pinned in by the twisted metal.
"Wendy, are you all right?" she asked.
But there was no reply, she could see Wendy, but she looked like a rag doll slumped in the twisted metal.
"Hold still dear," a voice said, "you'll soon by out."
"Can you see my friend?" Ann asked.
"We'll have her out soon as well," the voice said.
It wasn't long before she could hear sirens from all directions, and firemen with all types of equipment arrived and started levering the car apart.
"This one's urgent," a fireman said pointing at Wendy.
And within minutes a large helicopter was landing on the motorway.

There was lots of noise, metal being bent and cut, people shouting, children crying, and more sirens.

Before long Wendy had been removed, still as a limp doll, and taken to the helicopter.
"Bad way that 'un," Ann heard one of the paramedics say, and another said "get her to the hospital quick and she may make it."

Poor Wendy Ann thought, would she live, would she be horribly scared, poor Wendy.

CHAPTER SEVENTEEN.

Tony had spent the whole day yesterday driving around the Didcot area, but had not found anything. When he got back, there was no sign of the girls so he assumed they stopped somewhere overnight.

They had, but not as he had expected. They were both in Princess Margaret hospital in Swindon.

He had just got up, when the phone rang, it was Ann.
"Stay somewhere nice?" Tony asked.
"There was an accident, and both Wendy and I were taken to hospital."
"Oh... how are you!"
"I'm okay. They say I can go home, but no one will tell me anything about Wendy, she was hurt worse than me."
"Is she all right?"
"I don't know. I've even tried phoning the hospital, but they wont tell me anything because I'm not a relative."
"I'll find out," Tony said "and I'll come down and get you."
"You try and find out and I will call you back," Ann said now being quite worried about Wendy.
Tony phoned the hospital and pretended to be Wendy's brother.
"As well as can be expected," was as much as he could find out. When he prodded for more information he was just told that there was a Doctors round in a while and if he was in later then just maybe the Doctor could tell him more.

Ann phoned back, but was no more relieved by what Tony could tell her.

A few hours later Tony was at the hospital, and after having a problem finding somewhere to park, eventually he managed to get in.

Where should he go first he wondered, to see Wendy or Ann. He decided that if he was going to pretend to be Wendy's brother, he had better visit her first, and he knew Ann would not mind.

He went to the main ward block reception, and was directed to the accident and emergency unit, and from there to a ward on the next floor up.

He went to where he was directed, but although there was a name tag for Wendy, there was no Wendy. He stood staring at the empty bed, when a nursing auxiliary came in and started to strip all the bed clothes off the bed.

Was he too late he wondered, dare he ask?

"Tony," the voice said.
And when he looked around he was relieved to see Wendy in a wheelchair with one of her legs in plaster.
"How did you know I could go home?" she asked him.
He couldn't say anything, he just rushed over and put his arms around her.
"I'm pleased to see you to," Wendy said surprised at the sudden show of emotion.

Tony helped her get her stuff together, and got her to his car, with the plastered leg up on the back seat.

Having made her comfortable Tony told her he was now going to get Ann.

"Is Ann here, did she come to visit me?" Wendy asked.
Tony didn't know what to say, but asked what she could remember of the crash. It turned out that Wendy had no recollection of the crash, or the day before. She assumed she had been on her own.

Tony quickly found Ann, and told her of Wendy, and before long they were on the M4, on their way back to the hotel.
"Tell us about yesterday?" Ann asked Tony. "What did you find?"

Tony told of his hunch that if you drew a line on the map from Poole to Peterborough, and divided it in half you would get the same point as a line projected from Oxford would cross the line.

He explained he had done this, and it came out at around Didcot. As Didcot was a railway junction, and the River Thames was not far away he could see several places on the map with two bridges.

He explained that he had tried Didcot itself, Culham, Steventon, and many places in the area. Some of the instruction parts lined up many times, you either had two bridges and a power line, or two bridges and a wood all in the right place.
"Do you think it is in that area now?" Ann asked.
"I don't know," Tony replied. "We need to sort out what the rest of the clues mean."
"Do you think we need to break that second coded part?" Wendy asked.
"I don't think so," Tony said thoughtfully. "It say's its an alternative solution, just in case he had to move it."
"One is enough to look for," Ann said.

While they drove along, Ann was looking at some of the maps Tony had in the car.
"Here's a likely spot," Ann said "in the Bladon area near Blenheim Palace, and another to the west out in the country, that looks even better."
"Any power lines?" Tony asked.
"No," Ann said, "but they only show the ones with steal towers on the map."
"Let's go and see," Wendy said. "I could do with an outing."

So they visited the Woodstock area, Charlbury, Bladon and Witney being the larger places, but visiting many villages in between, before moving on to Lower Heyford, and then to many places to the west of Oxford. Several times they thought they had found a match, like on the A465 north of Kingston Bagpuize, and on a small road between Buckland and Bampton.

They kept their eyes open, and investigated every possibility they could find, moving south to the Reading area.
"There are far too many possibilities," Tony said. "Every place with a road, rail, river or canal combination gives the possibility of a match."
"We have covered part of one map," Ann said in agreement, "and there are over 200 maps. You need a team of people to do it this way."

Reluctantly they decided that hit and miss with a map was not the answer, and that they needed to solve all the clues, and look for a pattern, or something else to get them to the area. It was clear, they felt, from the notebook and the decoded clue, that information was being provided to get them to the start.

Over the next few days Wendy could not work while her leg was in plaster, so having nothing else to do decided to crack the second coded piece. This the notebook made clear was a reserve or secondary location just in case one was needed. The notebook was clear, while the first code was easy to break, the second was not. Wendy tried all different ways, and was about to give up when she thought of two more possibilities. "I will try them and then give up," she said to herself.

The first of these made it make more sense, and the second made it clearer. The crafty old wotsit, she said, using several tricks together.

She was able to show Tony and Ann, and confirm that all the information was the solution to the last part of the alternative.
"That means, the clues we have, give both the start for the initial or main and alternative solutions," Wendy explained.
"The same point," Tony said in amazement.
"No, not necessarily, I think it's some sort of shape with the centre, or several centres being the starting points."
"You've lost me," Ann said looking confused.
"Think of an oval," Wendy explained. "You draw it by having two points and a piece of string."
"Isn't that about as much use as saying a paper bag has an inside and an outside?" Tony said also having by this time forgotten what the conversation was about.
"That's an idea," Wendy said, "a reflection."
The other two looked at each other wondering if it was Wendy going mad, or if they were as dumb as they felt.
"No, look," Wendy said. "Draw a shape, a triangle or a square, and find the centre. That gives one solution, pick up that shape and flop it over that gives another."
"You start on the inside and I'll start on the outside," Tony whispered to Ann, and they both chuckled.
"Poole and Peterborough are two points," Wendy said,

"now find a third and possibly a fourth."

They went through all the clues again, and tried several possibilities without any idea of what they were looking for.
"Now let's try the outside," Ann said. "Let's look at where we haven't been."
"Okay, I'll close my eyes and tell you what I can see," Tony said walking into the furniture.
"Careful Tony," Wendy shouted, "you don't want to break a leg as well."

The intercom went, Ann was needed in the hotel, and they all made their way across. Several of the staff were concerned that Oliver Robson was selling raffle tickets in the bar.
"First prize, a weekend at the Hilton," he was saying.
"Can I see that?" Ann asked, and was shown the tickets.
"In aid of charity," Oliver explained.
Tony looked suspiciously with Ann.
"You'll have to sell a lot of tickets won't you?" Ann asked.
"Yes, but I will.... want to buy some?"
"No thank you," Ann said not quite sure what to do. "How much goes to charity and which charity?"
"Haven't decided yet, I was waiting to see how it goes."
"The Oliver charity is it?" Tony asked.
"No, it's like charity Christmas cards, a percentage will go to charity."
"But what percentage?" Tony pressed.
"Well... probably about 5%," Oliver said and made a move to continue selling.
"I don't think I can allow them to be sold here," Ann said.
"Oh, go on, it's for charity."
"The best room at the Hilton," Tony replied. "That would cost a fortune."

"I'll have one," said a lady listening. "I could do with a weekend in London."

Oliver took her money and gave her a ticket.

"So if I get the London yellow pages and call the Hilton, they will confirm the booking, and they will know of this competition?" Tony asked.

"Never said anything about London," Oliver said looking worried.

"Where then?" Tony asked.

"Well... well... actually it's the Pavilion Hilton on the M6."

"Do they have rooms?"

"Yes, there's a motel."

"You're definitely not selling them here," Ann said forcefully. "And if you don't put them away I shall ask you to leave the hotel."

Oliver reluctantly put them away, muttering something about stifling free enterprise, and made his way out of the bar.

Wendy was feeling the strain of standing, so made her way back to her flat, but as she left she looked at the others and mimicked counting her fingers, "what did I tell you," she said.

Mickey Jessett allowed Oliver to leave before coming over to Tony and Ann.

"Hi," he said. "I heard you had an accident?" looking at Ann.

"Yes, unfortunately I'll live," Ann said sarcastically, and scowling.

"Do you know that guy?" Tony said still looking at Oliver.

"Well sort of, Meldrum has seen him several times, and sometimes there are angry noises, but we have all been told to keep away."

"Meldrum into protection as well," Ann said sarcastically, "mind out or you'll miss your cut."

"I try to do a difficult job the best I can," Mickey said getting a little fed up with the constant criticism. "Can't we start again, and try to be civil to each other."
"Okay, now how can I civilly help you?" Ann asked.
"Well it's not help me, it's Miss Lewis, you can help her by getting her to co-operate. It looks suspicious when a possible suspect doesn't co-operate."
"She was injured," Tony interrupted. "In the car crash, and really did loose some of her memory."
"She should still co-operate," Mickey insisted.

On their way back to Tony's flat, Ann asked, "how would you like a weekend away at the Hilton. Quite cheap if it's the motel on the M6 you know," and they both laughed.

CHAPTER EIGHTEEN.

Two months passed, Wendy had completely recovered, and they had spent as much time as possible following up clues.

There was one which started; 'your knowledge of the country would be greatly improved', and ended with 'with your eyes open', and in between was just a long list of towns and cities.

A similar one that followed was more difficult it said; 'the following places may justify further inspection; Uxbridge, Stroud, East Bergholt, Goring, Hamworthy, Overton, Salisbury, Truro, Preston, Oxton, Inkpen, Nash, Tiverton and Stoneybridge.'

The second group presented more of a problem, as quite a few of these were place names that appeared in several different places, several four or more times.

They visited them all, including all variations of the second list, and even when they spotted that East Bergholt and Salisbury were linked by the painter John Constable they studied each of his paintings, and visited some more places. They found several or even more were on rivers, but aren't all towns, and several other common features. So far nothing was leading them, as far as they could see, any closer to the treasure.

The value of the treasure was now of less importance. It was them against the notebook, a personal challenge, and having put in so much time, they were not going to be beat.

THE MANY TOWN CLUE

Your knowledge of the country would be greatly improved by visiting; Penzance, Cleethorpes, Malvern, Willesden, Bletchley, Littlehampton, Rhyl, Worcester, Gloucester, Bradford-On-Avon, Chesterfield, Southport, West Bromwich, Wokingham, Bilston, Hazel Grove, Eastleigh, Sandown, Darlington, Bridgwater, Chorley, Wolverhampton, Fleetwood, Lichfield, Beverley, Slough, Runcorn, Ipswich, Washington, Brighouse, Colchester, Witham, Gillingham, Middlesbrough, Bideford, Taunton, Pontypool, Knaresborough, Torquay, Brixham, Coventry, Winchester, Harrogate, Nuneaton, Leek, Trowbridge, Newport, Lincoln, Stratford-upon-Avon, Caerphilly, Cwmbran, Whitley Bay, Keighley, Redditch, Great Yarmouth, Stockton-on-Tees, Lytham, Middlewich, Stockport, Carlisle, Conwy, Wigan, St Ives, Rushden, Bath, Skelmersdale, Leyland, Paignton, Smethwick, Chatham, Christchurch, Wellingborough, Honiton, Portsmouth, Dronfield, Swanage, Margate, Newton Abbot, Stowmarket, Chelmsford, Chichester, Windsor, Guildford,

On the romantic side, well, nothing had really happened worth telling you about. They enjoyed each others company, Wendy teased a lot, but so much effort was going into finding the treasure that there wasn't much time for anything else.

A meeting was planned for this afternoon in Tony's flat to discuss progress and where they should go from here. They had all arrived, and were sitting down with a cup of tea.
"Well," Tony said "what next?"
The two girls looked at each other, and there was a short silence before Wendy spoke. "We have been to so many places, seen so much, and have so many notes, I think we need to get it all organised."
"And then do it all again?" Tony said looking worried.
"No, just so we can make some pattern out of all the information we have."
"Any ideas how?" Ann asked, filing systems not being an area she was good at organising.
"Well," said Wendy. "I think we need three things, a ring binder with a sheet for each place, a card index by subject and a clue sheet to collect all the clues together on."
"A big job," Tony said, not liking paperwork at the best of times, "can you explain the card index?"
"Sure," Wendy was getting more confident now. "Say you find something Roman in a city you would file a card under Roman, and of course anything else you discovered. Later you can look through the cards and pick out piles of cards on a subject."
"Will that help?" Ann asked. "It seems a lot of work."

They discussed how it would work, and as it was Wendy's idea they all decided Wendy should organise it, but Ann did volunteer to write up each of the places they had visited.

The Many Town Clue contd...

Newquay, Grimsby, Warwick, Norwich, Maidstone, Tenby, Chester, Chester-le-Street, Woking, Folkestone, Maidenhead, Kidderminster, Stourbridge, Reading, Leigh, Wednesbury, Braintree, Barnstaple, Ramsgate, Northwich, Maldon, Leighton Buzzard, Keswick, Hove, Hanley, Dover, Bishop Auckland, Rugby, Ludlow, Henley-On-Thames, Billingham, Dudley, Godalming, Stoke-on-Trent, Derby, Blackpool, Durham, Cheltenham, Formby, Ashford, Bognor Regis, Exmouth, Pembroke, Southend, Dunstable, Bolsover, North Shields, Cheadle Hulme, Leamington Spa, Falmouth, Rochester, Newcastle-upon-Lyme, Halesowen, Scarborough, Lewes, Bournemouth, Lowestoft, Carmarthen, Hythe, Andover, Hinckley, Ripon, Neath, Seaford, Llandudno, Bradford, Lancaster, Plymouth, Halifax, Accrington, Kendal, Manchester, Holyhead, Swansea, Leicester, Bowness-On-Windermere, Hull, Canterbury, Ilfracombe, Abington, Port Talbot, Havant, Eastbourne, Warrington, Felixstowe, Bolton, Bromsgrove, Brighton, Bridlington, Aberystwyth, Blackburn..... with your eyes open.

Wendy created a card with all the main clue solutions which she hoped might jog their memory, or give them an idea. Each item had a number, and a solution.
"Later," she explained "we can add more", as there were still a few places to visit. Tony, you will notice had kept quiet and avoided any of the paperwork he hated so much.

They had nearly finished when there was a knock on the door, and answering it Tony was surprised to see Claire, and her baby.
"Hi, is it convenient?" Claire asked.
"Come on in," Tony said, "this is Ann and Wendy."
An older man followed Claire in.
"This is my Grandfather," Claire explained, "he brought me down to see you."
They talked for a while on what Claire was now doing, the treasure hunt, the documented filing system they had just devised, and several other things before a call came through on the intercom calling Tony over to the kitchen to sort out a problem with a delivery.

Once Tony had left, Wendy asked Claire about what had happened in Peterborough, and was told the full story.
"And you never knew him before?" Wendy asked.
"No, wish I had," Claire replied.

Claire's grandfather was looking out of the window. "I recognise that man," he said.
"Oh... that's Oliver Robson," Ann said having looked.
"Oh no it isn't... I just can't think of his name," he said thoughtfully, and explained that he had been a police sergeant until he retired recently, and that the man was known to him as a small time crook.
"A cross between Arthur Daley and that antiques dealer on

the telly," he said.
"He is an antiques dealer," Ann said pointing out of the window.
"I always count my fingers to make sure they are still there when he's around," Wendy added.
"Right on the borderline that one. Not big enough to be put away again, once was though, but not good enough to take your eyes off."
"Meldrum will fit him up, or his wooden top," Ann said sarcastically.
"Yes, that's it," the man said. "Kenneth Meldrum, known as Kenny, that's his name."
Ann and Wendy looked at each other, but didn't say anything.
"Yes," the man continued. "His father's a copper, but a bad one I hear, like Kenny, they say he's right on the borderline, but they put up with him because he gets results."
"Two crooks," Ann said looking at Wendy.
"No, I didn't say that," the man said. "They are different, the father does what he thinks he has to for the sake of society, while the son does it for himself."
"No excuses," Ann snapped. "There should be one law for all."
"Ah.." the man said. "There are so many laws, you can't enforce them all, and you have to police according to the person."
"How?" Wendy asked.
"If I was dealing with a 'yobo' who had a habit of taking and driving away."
"Nicking cars," Claire interrupted.
"Yes... I would not be over concerned about his tax disk or tyres, as long as it was his own car. Better he drives his, than take someonelses. But you Miss," he said pointing at Ann, "if you had a bald tyre, I would nick you, so you know you had to stay within the law, and didn't end up like him," he said waving out of the window.
"Blimey," Ann said. "I never thought of it that way."

"The deterrent effect, like having a nuclear bomb," he explained. "It's the police's biggest weapon."
"What?" asked Wendy, imagining police blowing up motorists.
"Well take business," he explained. "When one goes broke, we go in with the fraud squad, and dig, don't need much, just the smallest spot of dust and we prosecute. You see this keeps the rest in order."
"Why not go after the crooked ones instead?" asked Wendy.
"You do if they are very bad, but in most cases it would cause people to loose jobs, and do more harm than good, so we go for the deterrent."
"So you agree with hanging?" Ann said, feeling the previous explanation was unjust.
"Yes, best deterrent," the man said.
"But, what if it turns out it was the wrong man who was hung?" Wendy said thinking of cases over recent years.
"A problem, I agree, and that is why the police only want to hang people shooting policemen."
"Oh..," said Ann getting annoyed. "You want a deterrent to protect yourselves, even if its the wrong person, and blow the rest of us."
The man laughed, "see what a problem it is, from what you have just said, you want a deterrent, but you don't want to take the risk of hanging innocent people."

This man was Tony's guest Ann thought, I had better not tell him what I think, perhaps I can change the subject.
"Do you want to help Tony with the treasure hunt?" Ann asked Claire.
"Sure... but with a baby."
"No, what I have in mind is desk research," and Ann explained to her the card system, and suggested she look up everything she could find out about every town and create loads of cards. Wendy could then add them to the system.

Claire agreed to do this, both glad for something to do, and to help Tony.

The next arrival was Mickey Jessett. He had been around many times trying to persuade Wendy to give a statement about the South Wales murder. This had not been a good day, and he was getting a little fed up with being sent around again and again. Silly little idiot he thought as he approached the door, serves her right if they arrest her for this murder.

Having been shown in, he turned to Wendy.
"Come on Miss, we have to have a statement, and if I don't get one, I'm going to arrest you and take you down to the station and chuck you in a cell for a few hours."
"Hang on there constable," Claire's grandfather said. "You can't arrest her, unless she has committed an arrestable offence. You should also tell her, before you press for a statement that she has the right to have a solicitor present."
"Oh.. sorry sir.... I didn't realise you were her solicitor," Mickey said feeling like a little boy caught with his fingers in the sweet jar.
"I'm not, but if I were, I'd be filing a complaint right now."
"Oh... do you mind telling me who you are sir?"
"I'm your judge son, and if you don't behave, it'll be you in trouble."
A judge Mickey thought, blimey, now I've put my foot in it.
He explained he had had a bad day, apologised over and over again, and got out as soon as he could.
"Well that put him in his place," Ann said. She was pleased to see someone give Mickey a hard time.
"You're not a Judge Grandad," Claire said.
"No, I didn't say I was, I said I was his judge."
"Are you people trained to play with words?" Wendy

asked.
"No, its just a skill you pick up, lots of interviewing, and trying to catch people out. Frankly I'm glad to be retired."

A couple of days later, Wendy was in her flat when the telephone rang.
"Hello, Miss Lewis is it?" the voice said, she didn't recognise it.
"Yes."
"You don't know me, but I know who killed your boss."
"Who?"
"Sorry, I can't say, I'm... um... related you see... to him."
"Oh... so why call me?"
"Well, I want to make sure some evidence gets given in...."
"Yes!"
"And I've heard you're not scared of them, rumour has it you have a judge as a friend."
"Um..", Wendy said, it's not Mickey Jessett's voice.
"So I want you to get it and turn it in, so the police can arrest the man, and I won't be involved."
"Okay.." she said hesitating. She wasn't sure this was such a good idea.
"Right I will tell you were to get the stuff, and you hand it in.... will you promise to hand it in?"
"Yes."

The man on the phone gave Wendy instructions, she had to be on her own, but he assured her she would be safe, on a main road, and explained a bag would be hid by the first turning to the right, a track, on the road between the A470 and Aberdare, once past the first road on the left. The pickup was arranged for the following morning.

Wendy did not tell the others, they may have tried to persuade her not to go, or have even told the police.

She arrived at 8.30, in the morning, the time Wendy had insisted on, because the road would be at it's busiest, and she did as instructed. Went past slow the first time, went to Mountain Ash and turned, stopped, and looked around without getting out the car, on the way back, going back to the A470 island and turning. The traffic queues at the island were bad this morning, and every second seemed like an hour. Eventually she got to the island and was back on the road. She slowed as she approached the track, and signalled across, moving over into the middle, and then into the track when there was room.

She looked around, seems safe enough she thought, but just to be sure I will jump out and grab it quickly, and get off. So she turned the car around, and got as close to the point as she could. She then jumped out the car, sprinted to the spot with the red rope, grabbed the bag, and was quickly back in the car and away.

Rather than risk the island traffic, she decided to turn right down by the Rugby ground, and have a look at what she had picked up. She was hardly around the corner when police cars seemed to come from everywhere. They had blocked the road behind and in front.

A voice came over a metal sounding tanoy from one of the police cars.
"Armed police, throw out your weapon, and your bag, put your hands on your head and get out slowly."
Wendy looked around. Who were they talking to, but there was only her car between them. It had to be her.
"Come on Miss," the voice said. "You can't get away, so just give up and no one will get hurt."

She did as instructed, and once she was stood outside

several of them approached her slowly with guns outstretched and when they reached her, threw her roughly on the floor, before quickly searching, and handcuffing her.

"I'm arresting you for the murder of Paul William Patton," said the larger policeman without a uniform.
He was a frightening figure, and went on to say much that didn't sink in. I wish Tony was here she thought, and at the first opportunity said she wanted to see a solicitor.

She had been booked in, finger printed, searched again, this time by a woman police officer who could have made the rugby team, and put in a cell.

Some time later a solicitor arrived, with lots of forms to complete, so he could get legal aid to pay him to look after her, and he sat in while several officers tried to bully her into confessing.

The solicitor, she felt was not a lot of help, he never once intervened, just sitting making notes. They were all talking, trying to confuse her, all against her. No-one was listening to what she said.

"I'm not saying anymore," she said eventually, feeling really confused.
"Ten minute break, turn off the recorder," the big Detective said.

In the break she talked with her solicitor, and made him promise he would telephone Tony, and let him know what had happened.

The questioning went on all day, and only stopped at lunch time while they all went to lunch. Although Wendy was put in a cell of course, and given a sort of cold stew, it looked awful, as if someone could have eaten it before and brought it back up.

The afternoon session continued until 5pm, when the solicitor said he had to go for another appointment. Again Wendy was put in the dimly lit cell.

The cell was, it would appear, designed as a psychological weapon. As Wendy studied it, she could see why people confess to things they haven't done. Anything just anything to get out of this place. It smelt of cheap disinfectant, was bare except for a bench fixed to the wall and floor. On the bench was a thin plastic covered mattress. The bench was cleverly designed, so that when you sat on it your feet could not touch the floor, and in no position could you rest your back against a wall. If you sat back against the back, then part of your legs went uncomfortably over the edge, and if you picked up your knees, then the plastic mattress was guaranteed to slip.

Beside the main cell room, there was a small cubical off the side, with a toilet in it. It had been cleverly arranged so that the whole room and cubicle could be seen from the door, which was metal lined, and had a small hole at about head height, covered from the outside by a flap. Next to the door was a bell push, and above the bench high up, a window covered with bars, and frosted so heavily that it was difficult to even make out if it was night or day, especially as a street lamp stood nearby. Voices could be heard, and large doors clanging.

If only they had left her watch, or something to do, but no she had nothing. It was timeless, was it seconds or minutes passing, what time was it now she wondered; had Tony been told; would he be allowed to visit her?

She walked around the cell, tried sitting on the floor, tried using the mattress to make a chair, tried everything she could. She felt so alone, deserted in this terrible place. She would never have imagined it would be so bad, to be locked in a cell.

Time passed, and a lukewarm drink in a plastic cup arrived, and something she thought must have once been food. The drink, she could not make out if it was tea or coffee, but it was horribly sweet, they must have put ten spoons of sugar in here she thought.

She rang the bell, and after a period of time, she did not know how long, she had lost all sense of time, a policeman arrived and looked through the flap.
"Move back," he said, as he opened the door. "Yes what's up?"
"Can I have a pillow, and my watch?"
"No," said the officer slamming the door and walking away.

As she stood leaning against the wall, and tried everything she could think of to take her mind off time, she could suddenly understand why perfectly sane people would commit suicide in these terrible places.

She knew it was only a mix up, and of course they would let her out, but how terrible she thought for people sent to prison, especially if they were innocent, like her, she thought.

But what if they didn't sort it out. Would she have to spend the rest of her life in a place like this, would prison be better than this. She wondered, if she was going to end up there anyway, wouldn't it be a good idea to confess now, and get there quicker.

She rang the bell again. I'll confess to the murder she said to herself, anything to get out of this place. But by the time the bell was answered, she had thought more and realised they would not move her until the morning whatever she did.

Time passed slowly, she ached all over from standing in awkward positions, and tried to sleep. Then the drunks arrived and were put in nearby cells, they made so much noise, she could hear and smell people being sick. She could stand it no longer. She rang the bell.
"I want to make a statement," she screamed at the top of her voice.
"Pipe down, we haven't got time for your hysterics tonight," the voice on the other side said.
She fell in an uncontrolled heap on the floor, sobbing, hysterically crying.

Eventually she pulled herself together and made it to the bench. She slept for odd minutes, but was then woke up each time by people shouting, singing, being sick, or the thud of the heavy doors slamming.

I can hang myself with my jumper sleeves she suddenly thought, but there was nothing to hitch them, even the bars by the window were right against the glass, there was no way out.

The following morning Tony was woke up by the telephone, and was informed by the solicitor where Wendy was, and what had happened.

"When will they let her go?" he asked.
"Not much chance of that, they seem to have a good solid case," the solicitor said. "I wouldn't get involved if I were you," he said in a bored sort of voice, "she's going to be away for a long time."
"Oh. Can I visit her?" Tony asked not knowing what he could do to help.
"Doubt it," said the uninterested voice.

Tony noted down his telephone number and name, and as much detail as he could, and having told Ann what was going on, set off not for South Wales but for Peterborough.

You will know this is one of two initial books leading to treasure. A third book in this series will be available for somewhen in 1995.

It will be called:-

FAME OR FORTUNE

This book will start three years after the end of this one, and continue the story. The same characters are now involved in totally different situations. One is a wealthy writer unknown to the others, several now run a detective agency. You will also see the people you met in "To Search and Prosper", all now also three years older. While attempting to solve a variety of mysteries, and as they travel around remember parts of the treasure trail solution. Depending on what has happened with the Treasure Trail this could help reveal the original or alternate solutions.

It will be fast moving, exciting, amusing and you will find the unexpected happens.

Order your copy now, and have it sent to you immediately on publication.

The page size and binding style will match this book. The number of pages is not yet known.

Order at today's prices £14.95 post free from:-

Knowledge Base Publications Ltd
19 Penybryn, Mountain Ash,
Mid Glamorgan CF45 3TJ

Or write and ask us to tell you when it is available.

CHAPTER NINETEEN.

Tony reached Peterborough, and quickly explained what had happened, and Claire went with him, leaving the baby with her mother.

They arrived at Claire's grandfathers house just as he was leaving, but seeing their worried expressions he invited them in and listened intently to what Tony had to say.
"As I see it," Claire's grandfather said thoughtfully, "they have a threat, possibly giving a motive, opportunity as she has no alibi, and the Sunday working could have been a device for them to be alone, and evidence linking her to the event in that she was caught red handed recovering the items removed from the scene."
"Yes, but she didn't do it," Tony said.
"Well someone did, and most murderers are who you would least suspect."
"You've met Wendy," Claire interrupted, "do you think she would?"
"Strong willed, independent, a little immature possibly," her grandfather said thoughtfully. "You never can tell, and unless she has an alibi, or someone else confesses, it will be down to a jury to decide."
"But a jury would see she didn't do it," Tony said, but not very confidently.
"Barristers put their case, the prosecution first," explained Claire's grandfather, "and they will black her character as much as they can, will produce witnesses and drag it out for a couple of weeks, then it's the defences turn, but from what you say they haven't got any defence, then comes the closing arguments, and the jury convicts."
"Oh" said Claire, "there's no hope."
"There's always a chance," Claire's grandfather said, "Jury's

are often unpredictable, but being so attractive is a problem."
"Why?" Tony asked.
"Well the women will be jealous of her appearance, and the men will feel if they were her boss, they know what they would try."
"Oh, I see, so what do you suggest.... will I be able to see her?" Tony asked.
"Yes, once she's charged, and remanded, she will be able to have visitors."
"What about now?" Tony interrupted.
"Well.... well I shouldn't tell you this, but there is one way."
"How?"
"Well if the police don't know you, you could persuade her solicitor to take you in as his assistant or clerk."

They talked for a few minutes, and Tony took Claire home before setting out for South Wales. Claire as you would expect offered to help in anyway she could, and asked to be kept informed.

By the time Tony got to South Wales it was mid afternoon, and he had to wait in the solicitors office until about 4.30pm for the solicitor to come back.

It was five minutes to five before Tony was shown in, and he was told just about word for word what he had been told on the telephone.
"Can I see her?" Tony asked.
"They haven't charged her yet, but I think they will tomorrow morning."
Tony explained about coming in as his assistant, but the solicitor wasn't sympathetic, and wouldn't even consider it.
"You can see her tomorrow afternoon I expect," he said

several times.

Tony made his way back to the hotel, and on the way heard on the radio, that someone had now been charged for the murder. Oh well he thought, at least I will be able to see her now.

Back at the hotel, news of the charge had been heard. One of the staff friendly with Jeanette Wilson, the receptionist that had previously gone off with her boyfriend, but who had since returned to the area, had called her to tell Jeanette her old job would be available.

Jeanette was with Ann, when Tony arrived, and Ann explained to Tony that she had no option but to give Jeanette another go, as she desperately needed a receptionist, especially as one of the others was ill.
"Look, I'll box up Wendy's stuff and put it in store," Ann said.
"No," Tony insisted "she'll be back soon."
"Tony," Ann said firmly. "It'll be months maybe a year before there's a trial, and we have to be realistic."
"Okay... move Wendy's stuff to my flat," Tony said, not wanting to admit to anyone that he might be fighting for a lost cause.

Wendy's stuff was boxed up and moved into Tony's flat. It appeared that only Tony thought Wendy was innocent, even Ann had doubts.
"After all, we don't know her very well," Ann had said, and "when you have been let down by staff as often as I have, you get well... a little sceptical."

Chapter Nineteen

Tony was convinced, totally convinced Wendy was innocent, and decided he would prove her innocence, after all someone had to.

Tony called Mickey Jessett, or rather he called his works number and asked that an urgent message be passed to him.

An hour or so later Mickey arrived, and Tony quickly told him what had happened.
"Solicitor won't be much help," Mickey suggested.
"Why?" Tony asked.
"Well, when someone kills a solicitor, another's sympathies are hardly likely to be with the murderer."
"But won't the police investigate, and look for an alibi," Tony said hopefully.
"Well if she offers one, they will check it out, but they won't go looking for something to help her."

They discussed the options, Mickey held out little hope that Tony could do anything useful to help.

Later that evening, Tony was in the hotel bar, and although he didn't usually drink much, tonight was an exception. He was mad with everyone, society, and even Ann for not believing in Wendy.

He was just sitting there staring into his glass, when Kenny, the man known by everyone as Oliver Robson, came over.
"Bad luck about your mate," Kenny said. "I bet your feet get cold nights now?"
"She didn't do it," Tony said.
"Course not, and anyway this is Britain, everyone's

innocent until proven guilty."
"She didn't do it," Tony repeated.
"She didn't until it's proven," Kenny said. "I'd fit her up with an alibi, if I were you."
"How?"
"Say she was in your bed at the time, or find someone else who for a few readies will."
"No, that would never work."
"Might, I could find someone for you, for a little commission of course," Kenny said, always looking for a little earner.
"No, I'll prove she didn't do it."
"I see, your going on the radio, and TV and going to persuade the real murderer to come forward are you."
"No, but I could do a radio appeal," Tony said sitting up, "I could launch a campaign."
What a fool he thought, drinking wont help, it's action, what would Wendy say, get organised, draw an action chart or something.

Tony went back to his room, and got out a pad. Now what can I do. But although he thought, and thought the pad remained blank, there was nothing he could think of to do.

The following day Tony did see Wendy, although it took him some time tracking down exactly were she was. Wendy was of course absolutely delighted to see him, the solicitor having forgotten to say he had seen Tony, she thought even Tony had given up.

After a little cry, she told him of all that had happened, of the cell, of all the questioning.
"It's all now up to a barrister," Wendy said. "I reckon I need a good one."
"We'll find the best," Tony said, hoping he could.

Before leaving he told Wendy that she had to list for him everything she did on the day the murder took place, in exact detail, right down to when she went to the loo, and even anyone she remembered seeing, even if she didn't know them or know who they were.

She told him briefly what she had done, but said she would write it all down for him to collect in two days time.

Before going back to the hotel, Tony went up to Aberdare, over into the Rhondda valley, and round to Treorchy and over the mountains to junction 36 on the M4. He didn't notice much of the journey, he missed the stone circle in the middle of modern houses, the views from the top of higher mountain tops, and just couldn't help thinking of Wendy. He drove to the Welsh Folk Museum at St Fagans, but didn't go in, and back to the M4, arriving at junction 32, stopped for petrol that he didn't need, before going back to Aberdare.

The purpose was to get some idea of the time it would have taken, and where Wendy would have been at each time. He instinctively drove to the house where his relation had lived and stopped outside.

He was just sitting and thinking, when he noticed an elderly lady up the road waving and beckoning him. Thinking it may be something to help Wendy he jumped out and went over to her.

She explained that she had seen him come before, and had afterwards been told who he was, and of the treasure hunt.
"Have you found it yet love?" she inquired.
Tony explained he had been chasing all over the country, had now solved most of the clues, but so far had no idea

where the treasure was.
"I've got a couple of ideas," the lady said.
"Oh.. what?" Tony asked, really still thinking of Wendy.
"Well he used to always have a summer holiday each year in the New Forest," she explained. "A place called Wootton near New Milton, he told me, a cottage he stayed in, every time, a place that used to be a post office, it was, right back to the time the penny post was introduced."
"Oh.. that's interesting," Tony said making a note, and wondered what Wendy would get for tea, perhaps he thought, he should have got some food and sent it into her.
"And do you know where he was brought up?" the lady asked. And before he could answer, "it was a place cow something a funny name, he told me he lived in a thatched cottage, one of those that is now a thatched pub."
"Oh," Tony said making a note. He hadn't heard that before.
"When he was younger," she continued, "the thatch on the house next door caught fire, and there was a mad scrabble, there was 11 boys and 3 girls plus the parents in then, and they all had to get out, and a horse drawn fire engine arrived, and put it out."
"Sounds exciting," Tony said, not really listening.
"He often went back there, used to plan his trips by rail, so he could stop at something junction."
"Honeybourne," Tony said.
"Yes, that's it."
Tony thanked her for the information, and made an excuse to get away, maybe he would come back another day he thought.

Tony made good time getting back to the hotel, and updated Ann on all that had happened. He would visit Wendy again the day after tomorrow, he told Ann, who was more interested in what he had learnt from the lady in Aberdare.

"You have to face facts," Ann told him sternly. "Wendy has little chance, with the system as it is. If she had told us last week she had done it, we could have given her some money to get out of the country."

"But she didn't do it," Tony said, wondering why no one except him believed in Wendy's innocence.

Tomorrow he would do something he thought.

CHAPTER TWENTY.

That night Tony got very little sleep. He found the thought of Wendy being caged up for a single night totally repulsive, yet it could be for years. No one except him seemed to care, and he didn't feel confident in his own ability to help.

Eventually after much thought, he decided two things needed to be done. He had to try to find an alibi for Wendy, and get the best help for her he could. This would need money, and he knew how to get it didn't he; the treasure.

Up to now the treasure hunt had been a game, him against the notebook, but now it became serious, urgent, something to be conquered straight away.

The following morning he was up early, and had Ann up early as well.
"Come on, hurry," he told her. "We are going to Southampton."
Ann was pleased to see him looking a little happier. She didn't think they could do much for Wendy, so didn't see the point in making a lot of fuss.

By mid morning they were in Southampton, and had a look around they found Bugle Street, with old houses, and sections of the old town wall, and on the quay side they found god's house tower, originally part of the towns defence, but now an archaeological museum.
"What's the clue?" Tony asked.
"It say's; starting from the oldest surviving church in the

city, go towards France, right past the city walls, ahead about half a mile is the end, but this isn't the place."

They looked around the area, made lots of notes, and Tony explained what he thought the answer was, but Ann wasn't at all convinced.

"Looking on the map," Ann said. "Look there and over here."

And then Tony realised it wasn't what they had thought.

"He made a mistake with the clue," Tony said. "Look it's based on reading the map wrong."

"So you don't think he actually visited all these places?"

"Yes, he must have done, or had very good guide books, how else would he know which was the oldest church."

They discussed it at some length and decided that all the places must have been visited, but that he must have used maps and guide books as well.

"So what about that big list of towns and cities?" Tony asked.

"Well."

"Do you think he went to all of them?"

"Don't know, perhaps they are just added to slow us down."

"Where next?" Tony asked.

"That's it," Ann replied, although disappointed to have finished so soon.

"Well in that case I want to go to the New Forest and look at the Wootton area."

You may recall, this is where the lady in Aberdare had told Tony that John Pugh, the person who wrote the notebook, had taken his summer holiday each year.

They had no problem in finding Wootton, which was right on the edge of the New Forest, about two miles north of New Milton. They discovered that there was a disused railway line about a mile to the north of Wootton, and several roads crossed both this and a stream.

Stopping and looking at some wild ponies, and a large number of pieces of wood lying around, Tony said, "if he has hidden it in one of these logs, we may never find it."
"That's why we have the final part in such detail," Ann said, not wanting to admit that the size of the forest was enormous.
"Are there other areas like this?" Tony asked.
"Lots," Ann said with a smile. "There's lots of forests, like Sherwood Forest, Savernake Forest, and then there is all the National Parks, like Dartmoor and Exmoor."
"Blimey," said Tony looking around, "so we won't do it by just wandering about."

They found the area around and to the north of Sway particularly interesting, particularly the B3055 to Brockenhurst, which has a number of bridges. Following the instructions they thought it might lead them to what is known as the ornamental drive, and was interested to see everywhere around here that areas had names followed by inclosure. There is Fletchers Hill Inclosure, Poundhill Inclosure, Vinney Ridge Inclosure, and Rhinefield Sandy's Inclosure to name just a few.

"This is where I would hide my treasure," Ann said pointing to a point near the stream.
"What treasure?" Tony asked.
"Well the one someone will give me one day."

They spent the rest of the day looking around some of the villages, and looking at the houses. They spotted a large

thatched cottage at Sway, right on the edge of the forest, they both agreed it would make a perfect place for bringing up a family.
"Could you settle down here, and leave everything behind?" Tony asked Ann.
Was this a proposal she wondered, but looking at him, to her disappointment she could see it was just conversation.
"Oh. Yes," she answered. "Could you?" hoping to lead him onto the subject of marriage or even just living together.
"I think so, in a few years," Tony replied not realising the hidden meaning behind her question.
"Oh..." Ann said a little disappointed.
"Brandy Cottage," Tony said, "Game, from the forest and a Brandy liqueur."
"Drambuie for me," Ann added quickly.
"Okay," Tony said. "Time to think about something to eat."
"Yes, I'd be delighted to go out to dinner with you," Ann added even more quickly.
"Okay, let's find a nice place in the forest."

Which is exactly what they did, Tony had a medium rare steak, while Ann had veal. They both had black forest gateaux, and each had their favourite liqueur before driving back towards the hotel.

While still in the New Forest Tony pulled into a quiet side road.
"Well sir, what are we doing down here?" Ann said hoping it was going to be a night to remember.

Perhaps he wanted to check the map, perhaps he thought he had spotted the treasure, or did he have something else on his mind?

CHAPTER TWENTY ONE.

It was raining hard the following morning when Tony woke up. 9.30am, too early to get up, he thought, and then suddenly remembered Wendy.

What can I do that will not already have been done he wondered, will I make things worse for Wendy if I get her hopes up, and then let her down. Would it be better if I just went back to sleep?

He laid there thinking, would he do any good, and if he wanted to help would it not be a better idea to find the treasure.

That's the answer he thought, jumping out of bed. I'll go and find the treasure, and use some of the money to help Wendy.

He quickly got ready, got in his car and headed down the M4. Avebury was his destination, one of the few places in the notebook that he had not yet visited.

He would turn off at the first Swindon junction, and go through Wroughton to get to the road to Avebury.

As he approached the roundabout, he remembered the accident that had taken place on the next roundabout. That road also went to Wroughton he remembered, so decided to go to that junction.

As he drove he saw on the right Princess Margaret Hospital standing on top of the hill, and then as he approached the roundabout he noticed the Innovations factory unit, the people who send out those catalogues of new and unusual items. Good job someone tries new things he thought, and then thinking of Wendy, he thought perhaps I can add a new direction, or new ideas that could help, so he kept on going, until he got to where Wendy was being held.

He had to wait some time before he could see her, and when he did she looked terrible, sort of grey, lifeless, as if all the life spark had been drained away.
"Hi, how are you?" he asked, mainly because he couldn't think of anything else to say.
"Okay... I suppose," she said with no emotion.
"Did you create that list for me?" he asked.
"Here," she replied handing it to him.
"Oh.." Tony said looking at the few details. "Can't you remember anything else?"
"Not much."
"What?"
"Well, there was a family at the folk museum, I leant them my hanky when the little girl fell over."
"Do you know where they came from?"
"No, but I did see them at the services when I stopped at the Little Chef, so they must live Swansea sort of way."
"Or were taking the scenic way home. Can you describe them?"
"It's ages ago, I can't remember."
"Come on try, it might help."
"I can't," she snapped, now starting to get annoyed.
"You must, no one will believe this, we have to find them."
"Why don't you go away," she shouted. "You don't believe me. You don't have to come."
"But Wendy, I want to help."
"No one believes me, no one, and you're the same as the rest, just leave me alone," and with that she got up and left.

Well Tony thought, was that the real Wendy, or was it the

effects of this place. He had never seen her get so mad before, and he couldn't help thinking it's a good job she didn't have a gun.

He was here now, he would do the best he could. As soon as he saw a phone box he called the local radio station, and spoke to a researcher from a programme on later in the day. She agreed to talk over with the producer the possibility of an appeal to find the family that Wendy had seen.

Tony found the radio station, and managed to park nearby, and after a short while the researcher came down.
"Hi, I'm Andrea," she said. "We spoke on the phone."
"Any chance of doing an appeal?"
"Well... yes and no."
"Sorry!"
"Well you can't do a direct appeal, but we can interview you about your search for these people."
"Great!"
"But we have to be careful, there are subjudicy rules, and we don't want to be accused of trial by media or trying to influence a jury."
"Okay."
"And there's one other thing... um.... how do I put this. We have to turn over to the police any information we receive, good or bad."

Having had a cup of coffee, and told Andrea all he knew she went back to brief the presenter, and a little while later they invited him into the studio.

It was an unusual sort of room, with a large glass window you could see out. He was surprised to see the presenter had all the controls, discs, tapes, players, and piles of material. He had always imagined there would be an army of assistants, engineers, and production staff.

The presenter had a small computer screen, and he had seen a similar one on the desk Andrea was using just outside the studio.

They set up the sound volumes, with Tony saying some nursery rhymes, which made him feel a little silly. The presenter then went over the general format of what he was going to do. He explained to Tony that in a phone in like this, he, Tony would be able to hear and speak to callers using the headphone set. They tried this on, and he put an experimental call through to Andrea just to demonstrate.

With all his bank of switches the presenter really was in control, he thought.

At the end of the record Tony was introduced, and his search explained, he told them that Wendy had been at the Folk Museum, and had gone on to Asda, arriving at just before 5.30, too late to get anything as the shop was shutting. How she had got petrol in the services nearby, and come down the M4 to the main services by junction 36, the turn off to Bridgend. He explained the family he was looking for, and Wendy's meal at the Little Chef, and trip home over the mountains stopping at a high point to look at the views and get an ice cream, before entering the Rhondda Valley near Treorchy.

He had hardly finished speaking when the first call came on the line. He did not want to give his name.
"Oh, what can you tell me?" Tony asked.
"Well, it's a pack of lies," the man said. "Asda shuts at 5pm on Sundays, and if one part's a lie, you can bet your life the rest is."
"But it's not your life were betting with," Tony said.

And then the man went on about bringing back the death penalty. Luckily for Tony the presenter stepped in and rescued him.
"Well, we'll play a tune now," the presenter said, putting on a compact disc.
That's blown it, Tony thought, feeling totally discredited already.
"That was a lucky break," the presenter said smiling.
"Well, I thought it was terrible."
"No, a bit of conflict, or argument, and people start to take more interest."
"Oh."
At the end of the record, the presenter reminded everyone who was with him. Then over the next twenty minutes there were several other callers, one at first appeared hopeful, until he realised it could not be Wendy the person was referring to. Another was very negative, who said she had witnessed the meeting between Wendy and the family, but insisted it was another Sunday.

There were several calls for and against the death penalty, and eventually it was time to move.
"Any last thoughts?" the presenter asked him, still on air.
"Well, I have explained the family, and they may not be listening, could any of you who know of such a family please contact them."

Tony sat around in reception for another half an hour just in case there were any calls, but there wasn't.

What next he thought, and set off to drive around the area. He stopped part way up the A470 at Tesco's petrol station for fuel. Paying by credit card he stared at the credit card machine, it printed on a roll of paper three sheets thick, the top two being torn off and signed, and the bottom one still in the machine.

Yes, it had the time and date on it. He watched, while the copy still on the machine was rolled inside by the next transaction, and he was given one piece, and the other put in the till.

Fantastic he thought, perhaps Wendy used a credit card. Going into the Tesco entrance he found a public phone on the wall and called the hotel.

Ann was out, but he managed to get put through to one of his junior chefs. It took some persuading, but eventually he agreed to go over and break into Tony's flat to look for a credit card statement or receipts amongst Wendy's stuff.

Tony went for a walk around the store, and was impressed with the work of the on site bakery and the fresh fish counter display. He allowed fifteen minutes before calling back, and yes he had found her credit card information, and was able to give Tony the credit card number.

Next Tony phoned Claire and asked her to call the credit card company, and see if they could provide any information.

Another walk around, this time concentrating on the fruit and vegetables, and looking at the contents of the various tinned cook in sauces.

He then called Claire back, but unfortunately although she had explained everything to the credit card company they still insisted everything had to be kept confidential, although they had suggested Wendy could authorise her solicitor to get the information.

So back to the other petrol station by Asda, perhaps they had a roll of paper like the Tesco machine.

Tony stood and watched several people pay, and asked to see the receipt for one customer.

The credit card voucher was on a two part set, one part went in the till, and the other a green piece was given to the customer. Yes, it had the date and time, and off course the credit card number.

Seeing something unusual going on, one of the girls left one of the two tills to see what was going on. Tony explained what he was doing, and asked about the other part.
"I can do better than that," she explained. "Come over here."
Tony followed her to the counter.
"Not all customers want a VAT receipt, but we print them anyway," and she showed Tony a receipt, it too had the date, time, credit card number amongst the information.
"What happens if people don't take them?" Tony asked.
"We throw them away."
"Oh." Well that wasn't going to help.
"But look, there is a second copy in the machine, which is still on the roll."

She explained that the manager keeps these rolls, and before long they had found the receipt date, and there at 5.03pm on the Sunday was Wendy's card number.

Tony thanked them for the help, and asked them to keep it handy so the police would be able to see it.

They let him use the telephone and he called the police, having been put through to the right person he said, "I can prove Wendy was at the petrol station at 5.03pm."
"So," said the detective.
"So, her alibi is not a lie."
"Well she was there at 5.03pm, and the murder took place between five and six or thereabouts, but she could have been back in Aberdare by soon after 5.15."
"Oh," Tony said. That was disappointing.
While there he phoned the radio station and spoke to Andrea.
"There's been an interesting call," she told him, and went on to explain some people were making a home movie by a carvery in the Treorchy area, and had Wendy and her car on video. They could prove the date, and that she was going towards Aberdare at about 6.30pm.

Tony thanked her, and although he felt it was useful he knew what the police would say, she could have got back committed the murder and gone for a drive by then.

Tony drove down to the Little Chef on the services, perhaps Wendy had used her credit card there as well.

The people there were very helpful but no, there was no record of Wendy's credit card being used at the relevant time.

Well there was nothing else he could do. He had better go home, and explain to Ann why he had asked someone to break into his flat.

Driving back along the M4, he decided to just pop back into Cardiff and thank Andrea for all the help she had given him at the Radio station, he was surprised to be shown back into a studio, now with a different presenter.
"I've just popped in to see Andrea," he explained.

"Just a moment," the presenter said. "Please put on the headphone set."
Perhaps this is the only way to talk to Andrea when she is working, he thought.
"I have Tony Hyatt with me," the presenter announced over the air. "Have you had any luck?"
Tony explained what he had found out, but was not able to prove the middle bit.
"So you're giving up?" the presenter asked.
"I can't think of anything else to do," Tony replied.
"Perhaps we could take just one call."
"Oh... okay."
And once the person began to talk, he could see on the presenters face that he had known of this call. It was the mother of the missing family, yes she could confirm Wendy was at the Folk Museum, and at the services, yes all the times he wanted, and yes they had got petrol at the services and had a timed and dated credit card receipt.

There were tears streaking down Tony's face, he had done it, he had proved Wendy could not have committed the murder.

He didn't usually get this emotional, and he kept on apologising to the presenter and people at the radio station, but a lot of them by this time also had wet eyes.

"We have it all taped," Andrea told him, and I have dispatched a courier with all the details and a copy of the tape to the police.

Tony knew the police would want to check it all out, and it would be the following day at the earliest before Wendy was let out.

On the way home he suddenly thought of Oliver Robson, he had offered to set up alibis'. It wasn't him was it, it wasn't something he had set up, and..... and.....

CHAPTER TWENTY TWO.

That evening back at the hotel he explained all that had happened, to Ann. Who insisted, to his embarrassment, on listening to the tapes Andrea had given him.

Oliver Robson, was no where to be found. He had totally disappeared, which Tony took as a bad sign.

The following morning Tony phoned Wendy's solicitor.
"May take some time," the solicitor explained. "The police have a lot on, and well it's probably a hoax."
Not really the sort of person you need on your side in a crisis Tony thought.

Tony next called the police to find out what they were doing.
"It's all done sir," the officer said.
"And?" Tony asked.
"And it all checked out, so we will ask the court to release her."
"When?"
"About 2pm today in chambers."
"Can I pick her up?"
"Yes. If you want you can tell her, once the order has been issued."
"Oh great!"

Tony set off for a second day to South Wales. He arrived where Wendy was being held, and was shown into a little office, where he waited until news came that Wendy was to be released.

"Can she come now?" he asked.
"Do you want to tell her or shall we?" the officer asked.
"Oh can I!" Tony said.

A few minutes later Wendy was shown into the office. She looked totally confused, this was not where visitors visited people."
"Good news Wendy, you can come home," Tony said.
There were lots of hugs, and a few tears, and then Wendy went out to get all her belongings before being shown out.

She stood just looking at the traffic and the sky.
"You never realise how much you miss, just ordinary things, like traffic, birds singing, the wind on your face, until you have it all taken away," Wendy said squeezing his hand so hard, so it didn't get away.

As they drove back along the motorway towards the hotel, a road they had both got to know rather well, Wendy turned to Tony.
"Thank you," she said. "You got me out. Without you I would be like so many others, locked up for years for something I didn't do."
"Oh... that's all right," Tony said getting a little embarrassed. "That's what friends are for."
Wendy thought for a few minutes then she said, "you know in some cultures, if you save a life you own that person."
"Yes."
"Well, you saved my life. I would never have survived in there. So I reckon I belong to you now."
"A slave you mean."
"Yes, that's it, I'm your slave. You tell me what you want, and I'll do it."
"Anything!"
"Well... um.... well.... yes absolutely anything."

Tony thought for a few minutes, and lots of ideas flashed through his mind.

A little bit further on he pulled off the road at an island and found a place to park.

Reaching for a writing pad, he said "I've never had a slave before, so perhaps we had better get it in writing."
"What do you want me to write?" Wendy asked.
"Just what you said," Tony replied. "You're my slave, and you will do absolutely anything I ask of you."

She wrote it out.

"Thank you," Tony said taking it from her.
Having read it through, out aloud, Tony said "now I am ordering you to tear up this piece of paper, and with it destroy any commitment you have to me."
"But... but..."
"No buts, you said you would do whatever I told you to do, so come on honour your contract."
She tore it up, as instructed, and they set off again towards the hotel.

A little bit further along Wendy having thought about what had happened asked "why didn't you want me?"
"It's not you I didn't want," Tony explained. "It was the concept of you doing anything with or for me due to an obligation. At some time we may both decide on something, but you have to decide as an equal."
"Oh.. I see," she was relieved, but it was a pity he said at some time, which sounds like in the future. "How soon?" she asked.

"Wendy I like you, but today you're not emotionally stable with all that you have been through."
It sounds, she thought, as if he thinks I'm nuts, but only for the present. I will just be nice to him she thought, smiling at him.

Tony explained that she was back in his flat, and about the job, but Wendy didn't mind. Back at the hotel everyone was pleased to see her, and assured her they had always known she was innocent.

Tony didn't need to tell her this was not true, they were all trying far too hard.

She had to go through the whole event, time and time again.

Later that evening Wendy told Ann how horrid she had been to Tony when he visited her, and about the slavery contract.
"You knew he wouldn't go along with that," Ann said.
"Well I was surprised when he wanted it in writing."
"What did you expect then?"
"I don't know."
"You're lucky he didn't tell you to get out and walk home, after all that's what slaves do."

Ann was pleased that Tony had handled it all so well, and even more pleased that there didn't seem to be anything between Wendy and him. He had the sofa again, and was clearly not taking any offers Wendy may have suggested seriously.

The next morning Tony woke Wendy up, with breakfast in bed.
"All the luxury of your stay away, I don't want you to think bad of this humble establishment," Tony said smiling.
"Oh... you're spoiling me," she said still being part awake.
"Yes.. today we spoil you, so up you get, and decide where you want to go."

He sat on the side of her bed, and helped her eat her breakfast. Then after putting away the tray, came back in with a cold flannel.
"You wouldn't," she said diving under the bedclothes.
"Come out," he said. "Or I'll come in there and get you."

About an hour later they were dressed and ready to leave.
"Where do you want to go?" Tony asked.
"Maid Marian and her merry men," Wendy replied smiling, "Nottingham."
"On the treasure trail?" Tony asked. "But I want to take you out and spoil you."
"You will, and after all we'll be in the Sherwood Forest," and she gave a little chuckle.
"Oh!"

Off they went arriving at Nottingham for lunch, and found the Tales of Robin Hood Centre quite easily, not far from the castle, appropriately as it turned out in Maid Marian Way.

They entered and paid. They were directed to a room where a girl dressed in green stood, with a small group of other tourists. They were given green and silver cards, where the silver was scratch off areas. They went through a door and into an Old Inn, with animated life sized models and lots of noise. It was so realistic it was hard to remember it was make believe. Then the Sheriff of Nottingham's men came, and then they escaped with the aid of more people in green.

A sort of ride took you through various scenes, there was noise, movement and smell. Suddenly the Sheriff's men caught up, and thud, thud, thud, arrows just missed them and stuck in posts. They got away and ended up in Sherwood Forest at a feast.

Next after the ride, an exhibition area, with lots of things to look at and more questions to answer for their scratch cards. Upstairs, and another area, with even more displays to look at. Handing in their cards they discovered they were both outlaws, and joined up with Robin Hood and his men. The people in front were given a Royal Pardon.

More to look at, and another room where a film is shown. Tony could have sworn there was a ghost in the room, as at appropriate times the filing cabinet opened and closed all on its own, the answering machine and other things seem to behave just as if someone was operating them.
"What next?" Tony asked Wendy having forgot all about the treasure hunt.
"Let's do it all again," Wendy said, and they did, and no one thought about the treasure trail until they arrived back on the upper floor.
"Clues," Wendy said.
"What?"
"What do we need to know for the treasure trail?"
"It said; the first person to place Robin Hood in the period of Richard the Lionheart was, left - John Major, right - John Webster, or straight on - Robin Lion."
"It has to be the one in the middle," Wendy said chuckling at the thought of John Major being around in fifteen hundred and something.
"Here it is," Tony said pointing something out. "It was in 1521."

"What next?" Wendy asked.
"There's something about Thoresby Park and the alternate."
"Anything else?"
"Which town or city has the original of the earliest writing putting Friar Tuck in the story."
"I heard that," Wendy said quickly writing down the answer. They found out much more of course, like the Robehod surname dated from before 1300, and that a Robert Hod fled from justice in 1221, was a fugitive in 1226, and was once a tenant of the Archbishop of York.

Robin Hood had been a legend for centuries, and it was not until 1598, that in a play he first became a nobleman, as the Earl of Huntingdon. Probably the oldest form of the story was as a ballad, with probably the first story in about 1261.

Bringing it right up to date, Robin Hood is the worlds best known legend and even today criminals in America are sometimes called 'hoods'.

The shop had an enormous range of books, and all types of souvenirs. They bought several things including a souvenir guide, which not only told the story, but also showed how the exhibits and ride were built.

"Where to now?" Tony asked as they left.
"This was great," Wendy said. "How about spending the night in Sherwood Forest, just the two of us?"
"You mean a motel?"
"No, let's get some blankets and go and sleep amongst the trees."

It sounded fun, and they found a shop selling car blankets, and got a large sheet of plastic from a DIY shop just in case it rained.

"Open space, absolute freedom," Wendy said. "But do you want to see Thoresby Park first?"
"Oh. Okay..."

They left Nottingham, and before they reached the motorway spotted Thoresby Park on the right.

They were in the grounds of the park, just looking around when there was a bang, and Tony slumped over.
Spotting blood coming from his side, Wendy screamed, and hugged him.

CHAPTER TWENTY THREE.

A second gun shot was heard, but did not hit either of them. Tony groaned, and rolled over. Wendy had her arms around him, tears streaming down her face.

"Please be all right, please, please..... please," she whispered.

"Okay Wendy, that stings," he muttered. "I think we need an ambulance."
Wendy wished she had learnt some first aid, perhaps she should stay with him, perhaps she should get an ambulance. There was no one in sight.

She ran to the main gate of the park and stood in the road forcing a taxi to stop.
"I have a fare Miss," the taxi driver said.
"Oh, someone's been shot, have you got a radio?"
Seeing the urgency the taxi driver radioed for assistance, and his base, contacted both the police and ambulance services.

It took some time for the ambulance to arrive, through the traffic, but the police were quickly on the scene.

Tony could not tell them much. He had not seen who shot him, and could not think of anyone who would want to. They asked him about what he did, and joked about the food being so bad that one of the customers would shoot him. He had to ask them not to joke as laughing made it hurt worse.

He was whisked off to hospital and had the bullet removed. He had suggested Wendy went back to the hotel, or at least found somewhere to stay, but she sat in the hospital and waited. She did phone Ann to tell her what had happened.

By the time Tony could be visited, Ann had arrived, and both girls went in together.

Tony insisted he was perfectly all right, although in truth there was a lot of pain in his side, where they had to dig around to get the bullet out.
"Good job I had all those doughnuts," he joked.
"Why?" asked Ann.
"Well it was just extra padding that was hit."
"And I suppose it was raspberry jam coming out," Wendy said.
"Ah.. that's good," Tony said starting to laugh and then wished he hadn't.

Tony told Ann all about their day at Nottingham, and promised to take her somewhen.

Sometime later the police arrived, and asked the girls to leave for a few minutes.

"The bullet removed from you has been matched by ballistics to the South Wales murder," the detective told him.
"Why would anyone want to shoot me?" Tony asked.
"Not sure, maybe you know something, or maybe it was meant for Miss Lewis and they were a lousy shot."
"Is Wendy in danger?" Tony said sitting up.
"We don't know," the detective admitted. "All we can

suggest is that neither her or you go to any exposed places."
"What for the rest of our lives?" Tony said in surprise.

The police explained there was little they could do, as they had no idea who it could be. They said they would inform his local police, and Tony suggested they talk to Mickey Jessett.

"I think we should tell the girls," Tony suggested.
And they agreed, and one of them went to get them. By this time Claire had also arrived. Ann having called her on the way up.
"Three ladies concerned about your well being," the detective said in surprise.
"You mean no one would be concerned if you were shot?" Ann said sarcastically.
"Miss Lewis, I presume."
"Goodness," Wendy said, "with that ability of detection we should all feel safe."
"Easy really," the detective said feeling pleased with himself. "You see Miss Lewis has a justifiable grievance with the police."
"Yes, I do," Wendy said.
"Oh.... you're Miss Lewis... um.... I got it wrong," he said realising what an idiot it made him look.

Tony explained to all of them the theory of it being a bad shot aimed at Wendy, or something, and that there was a danger that the police could not eliminate.

When the police had left they discussed all the options.
"Jessett, I reckon is the prime suspect," Ann said.
"No, I think it's Meldrum," Tony said.
"Or it could be whoever murdered Mr Patton and framed

me," said Wendy.
"Yes, it definitely is that," Tony said going on to explain about the ballistic tests on the two bullets.

Claire asked if they thought the murder of the solicitor and the theft of the notebook was linked.
"Goodness," Tony said, "I never thought of that. You mean someone stole the notebook, killed Patton and now want's us out of the way."
"Jessett," said Ann.
"Let us agree," Tony said thoughtfully "that in this case it is likely to be either Jessett or Meldrum."
"You're a genius," Wendy said. "We worked that out a few minutes ago."
"So what can you do?" Claire asked.
"Set up a trap," Tony suggested.
"Too dangerous," Wendy said squeezing Tony's hand.
"Not if we are all there," Ann said.
"But not Claire.... sorry Claire," Tony said. "But with the baby if anything went wrong."
"Oh... couldn't I just stay in the car, or operate a radio or something," Claire said sounding disappointed.
"Well."
"Yes," Ann said masterfully. "If we set up a trap at Avebury we can use the stones as shelters, and Claire can drive backwards and forwards on the main road through, and hoot if she sees anyone with a gun."

They discussed at great length how they would set up the trap, how Claire would go down in advance and map the area, and work out the safest points.

They could leak information to both Meldrum and Jessett, by asking if they thought Tony would be safe on the day, or if he should ask for police protection.
A few days later Claire and her grandfather visited them all

in Tony's flat. He wasn't at all impressed with their plan, and insisted that they all wear bullet proof jackets he had obtained on loan.
"How about a suit of armour?" Tony joked.

Three days before the outing Tony called Mickey and asked if he needed to tell the Wiltshire police about the Avebury trip, and just to be sure the message would get through, Ann phoned Meldrum to say she thought it was silly for Tony to go to Avebury, and suggested he try to dissuade him.

When Claire arrived her grandfather was with her. I'm coming as well he insisted, but I will stay in the car with Claire.

They took two cars, Tony, Ann and Wendy in one and the other with Claire and her grandfather went ahead, and having checked out the area met them behind a supermarket in Calne.
"Do you know this pool is where oxygen was first discovered," Claire said pointing to the stream.
"Lucky that," Tony joked "or we would all be going around," and he mimicked a person struggling to breath.

This was of course partly show, as he was quite nervous. Not only for his own safety, but the danger he was putting his friends in.

The plan was set, Claire's grandfather would drive while Claire gave Wendy and Ann a lift, dropping Wendy at the public car park, and Ann within the stone circle on the main road at the north near the entrance to Avebury Manor.

Claire's grandfather gave them all whistles. "No hero's," he said "just blow your whistle if you see someone you know and keep your head down. They will run, and we can tell the police who it is."

Tony was to drive into the centre of Avebury and park near the shops in the small car park, and then walk around the ring, starting in the east, part of the section Ann could see, past the museum, church, and round the southern part of the ring back to the main road. The last segment was considered too dangerous so he would come back along the road to the pub in the centre.

They got in their cars, and were quickly at Avebury, and awaited Tony's arrival.

CHAPTER TWENTY FOUR

As Tony drove into Avebury, passing the main car park on his left, and seeing the avenue of stones going off to his right. He drove through the southern part of the ring, he looked around, and took the next left and within yards a right turn into the car park in the centre.

Having checked his whistle was at hand, and his bullet proof vest correctly fastened, he paused and hesitantly looked around before setting off.

Was this a daft idea he wondered, and how did they know a gun man would be frightened by whistles.

As he walked in front of the Red Lion, the pub in the centre, he paused, the road ahead had a lot of cars parked in it. Was it safe to go down there?

He decided it was not, so turned to walk along the main road to the north, after a few yards, he passed through a gate, and was in the field which contains many stones, with an enormous stone directly ahead.

Reaching the large stone he could see Ann across the road. She was stood looking in the opposite direction, where she expected him to come from, but was occasionally looking around. She spotted him with surprise and came over.
"Anything wrong?" she asked.

He explained why he had changed the plan, and they decided Tony would wait there behind the big stone for ten minutes so Ann could go on ahead.

Ann walked on, trying not to make it too obvious that she was looking for someone, but stopping occasionally, and walking right around one of the stones, and then over to the ditch. By now she could see a gate ahead, and old barns to the right. The first and largest was made of wood with a thatched roof, the next made of stone and tiled, and the third which was not joined to the other two was also of stone, but with a slate roof.

Ann cautiously went down the steps on to a track. There was someone 15 to 20 yards away leaning on a tree on the other side. She was relieved to see it was the village bobby with an anorak on. Having spotted Ann, he walked down the track towards the road.

The opposite way, the track turned and went between two of the barns. I'll just check around there Ann thought, walking between the barns. She could see a round building on the other side of an area of grass, and in the middle of the grass a muddy pond.

As she came out from behind the barn, someone grabbed her from behind, and put their hand over her mouth.

Initially she panicked dropping her whistle, then she stamped on the toe of the person behind, making him lose his grip. Struggling free and turning.
"Mickey Jessett, so it is you."
"Quiet and move on down there," he said pointing in the direction of the large barn.
She noticed he had one hand in his pocket.
"Or you'll shoot me," she said pointing to his concealed hand.
"Just move.... now," he said forcefully.
She didn't really have any option. She did as instructed, waiting for a chance to get away.

They went past the pond, past the door to the big barn.
"Turn right," he instructed.
"Behind the barn?" she questioned.
"Yes, quickly."

She looked as she walked around, there did not seem to be any way out. Old carriage sheds on one side, the big barn on another and a stone wall the rest of the way.

Was he going to shoot her round here she wondered. She looked at the stone wall, could she climb it if she got away, could she get back through the big barn.

A large area of the rear courtyard was not visible, because of the barn, and walls, and one of the big doors was open on the back of the barn which hid more.

Perhaps she could get through the barn door, but she had seen Mickey run before, he was fast.

A little further round she spotted in the concealed part of the courtyard a police Rangerover. At first she thought it was something Mickey was using, then she spotted some officers leaning on it drinking something from a flask.

She ran as fast as she could towards them. Surely Mickey wouldn't shoot now, surely he would run away. Looking around she could see him catching up.

Her heart was beating violently, she was terrified. She tried to call out but no noise came out. He was now right behind her.

The officers stopped and looked.
"He's got a gun," she managed to shout.
The officers took cover behind the vehicle. Two of them had rifles.

Why didn't they help her, or didn't they realise she meant Mickey.

She reached the police Rangerover and tried to explain to the concerned officer that Mickey was after her. But partly through the confusion, and fear, and partly being out of breath, she didn't make much sense.
"It's all right, calm down," Mickey said. "No one's going to hurt you."
Surely he wasn't going to get away with this, she thought, I have to explain to the police.

By now she was more in control, and started to calmly explain, receiving no understanding but fits of laughter from all the officers present.
"Don't worry miss," a sergeant said. "The Chief Inspector won't hurt you."
"He's not a Chief Inspector, and he will," Ann insisted. Why wouldn't these clots help her.
"Sit down and have a drink," Mickey said handing her a cup.
"Drugged is it?" Ann asked.
"I need to get back out," Mickey said to the sergeant. "Look after her, and keep her here out of danger."
"Am I under arrest?" Ann asked.
"No," Mickey said sympathetically, "and I'm sorry I frightened you, but I had to get you out of danger."
"You could have said," Ann interrupted.
"Oh yes, and you would have blown your whistle, and spoilt everything."

After Mickey had left, the sergeant explained that Mickey was a Chief Inspector. He was part of a special home office team used to sort out rogue officers or stations. She was told he was investigating Meldrum, and several others, but had set up todays operation in co-operation with Wiltshire

Police to give them some protection. It was he who had issued the bullet proof jacket she was wearing, and Claire's grandfather was working with them, and had a radio.

When she doubted this he told her to unzip the bullet proof jacket and notice the address of the store it came from. It said Home Office Special Task Force - Central Stores.
"So why did he grab me?" Ann asked.
It was explained to her that she would have given away his presence or could have become a target herself.

A few minutes later and two officers wearing anoraks were back, with Tony with them this time.
He explained to Ann, that he had been called between the barns by one officer, and another in similar dress to him had taken his place. A few minutes later Mickey returned.

"If it's not you, it has to be Meldrum," Ann said.
"It's not me or Meldrum after you," Mickey said.
"How do you know.... it's not Meldrum?" Tony asked.
"I bet he's not," Ann snapped sarcastically.
"Okay, I'll prove it," Mickey said picking up the radio from the rangerover.
He asked the operator to patch him through to a telephone, and asked for Meldrum's home number.
Within a minute or so, Meldrum answered, and Mickey made up some excuse, and fairly quickly finished the call.
"See," said Mickey.
"He's here," Ann said.
"Impossible, I just spoke to him, and you heard me."
"No, when you were talking, I heard a plane on the radio, and a plane flew over here at the same time," Ann insisted.
"Oh. Haven't you noticed," Mickey said as if speaking to a child, "that when you speak in a telephone, any noise where you are can be heard in the earpiece."

At that moment a shot rang out, and the police were rushing off. The radio told of a figure escaping in the direction of the avenue, and on a motorcycle on the road to the south.

It was clear after a few minutes that he or she had escaped. The substitute officer was hit and winded, but not hurt due to the bullet proof jacket he was wearing.

After a while they all returned, and Claire's grandfather's car came in, having collected Wendy from the car park.

"Well it's not Meldrum, Mickey, or any of us," Tony said, "so who does that leave?"
No one could think of anyone, although they still all thought that it may have something to do with the South Wales murder.
"But how could they know we would be here?" Wendy asked.
No one had an answer.

A little while later, they all dispersed, but Tony and the girls in his car, and Claire's grandfather and Claire in their's went down to the track in West Kennett where the motorcyclist was last seen before going along the A4 to the Wagon and Horses, a stone built inn with a thatched roof.

They parked in the small car park opposite, making sure there were no motorcyclists around before crossing the road, and the cobbled forecourt to the inn.

They got bar snacks, and drinks and went through to the beer garden behind. Tony was the first to spot Billy on the climbing frame, and soon spotted the rest of the Merryweather's nearby.

The Merryweather family had been touring the area, and had just by chance stopped here. A safe garden for the children having been a consideration.

They updated them on everything that had happened since they last met, and they all got on so well, and were so interested in the Treasure Trail that Tony invited them to join in the search. Alex's logical brain was a major attraction, but the fact he had offered to help, not expecting a share had also been a factor.

That afternoon they split into teams, Claire and her grandfather going back through Marlborough to look at Savernake Forest, the Merryweather's going south to explore Salisbury Plain. Tony, Ann and Wendy decided to look around the Avebury area a little better, and after all there was a clue here still to solve.
"By Avebury, take the route to the east past a thatched wall, is all the notebook says," Wendy said.
"I saw it," Ann said. "Or I think I did, it was by the church."
They set off at once to have a better look, and the huge stone circle at Avebury, and from the church yard they found a path that went by a thatched wall, and followed it down over some bridges.

They visited a long barrow, Silbury Hill, Windmill Hill, the Avenue, and the Sanctuary, as well as the surrounding area.
"6.30," Tony said. "Time to think about dinner."

"Oh good," Ann said, "where shall we go?"
"Ah. I know just the place," Tony said and set off.

They arrived at a small country pub.
"The Black Horse," Wendy said. "Why here?"
Tony didn't answer, just led the way.

In the lounge bar, Tony pointed out on the wall details of how the Cherhill Gang, was in 1776, a collection of foot pads or horseless highwaymen, who held up people on the hill, which is sited on the London/Bath road near Calne. This gang were unusual in that no one could explain them, or remember their faces. Their clothes could not be described as they did not wear any. The naked highwaymen were said to have no distinguishing marks. Nearby is the oldest of the nine Wiltshire white horses cut into the chalk hillside.

"Shall we go in?" Ann asked, pointing towards the restaurant.
"No not yet," Tony said looking towards the door.
They had a drink, and sat talking when Mickey Jessett walked in.
"Now Ann," Tony said. "I've invited Mickey along. I think we all should be more friendly with him. After all he is looking after us."
Ann wasn't sure at first, but as the evening went on she did perhaps feel he was not as bad as she had first thought.

They told him about the treasure hunt, and how the Merryweather family were now going to help. He showed a lot of interest in the Merryweather's, and why they had happened to be around.

They found out that Meldrum had been taking a lot of holidays in various parts of the country, and that he had a main telephone line, a fax line, and a mobile phone. Mickey asked them to keep to themselves, all they had found out about him today, which they all agreed to do. He pointed out that his life could be at risk if his cover was disclosed.

At the end of the meal, Mickey asked Ann if he could give her a lift home, and to everyone's surprise including his, she agreed.

It turned out that she still was not totally convinced he was not involved, and used the trip home as an opportunity to grill him further.

Tony on the other hand, took Wendy via the A4 to the M4 junction near Reading. Which gave him the chance to show her Savernake Forest. She was quite surprised and excited to see wild deer in the forest. Tony also took her down some lanes to find the Savernake Forest Hotel, and down a path, to the canal to show her the canal disappearing into a tunnel. It was quite romantic, but there were lots of insects, that decided they both looked tasty.
"I should keep more clothes on when there's all these insects about," Wendy commented.
"Goodness!" Tony said. "I didn't realise you were going to take them all off. Maybe we could be highway persons."
They laughed so much they both nearly fell in the canal.

CHAPTER TWENTY FIVE.

Over the next week plans were made for another attempt to trap the gunman. Of course he or she would now be prepared, having seen the police in Avebury.

At Mickey's suggestion they settled on Westonbirt Arboretum as a location, because with all the trees it would be easy to swap people.

It was decided, much to Wendy's annoyance, that only Tony and Ann would go.

The plan was simple, Ann and Tony would be seen entering the Arboretum, and then vanish, reappearing at the far end of a clearing having a picnic. Except of course that it would not be Tony and Ann, but two shop window dummies. Wendy was to be left behind as three still people would look suspicious, and because of her trim figure, the bullet proof jacket was far too obvious.

Mickey had a detailed plan of the Arboretum, and Monday was decided as a good day, partly because it fitted the current pattern of visits, and also because there would be less of the public around.

Wendy studied the plans, and could see no reason why she should not be allowed to come along. She was a little annoyed to find Claire's grandfather had suggested she be positioned in the car park at Avebury to keep her out of the way.

Chapter Twenty Five

They let everyone know of their plans, and on the following Monday set off early for Westonbirt, which is located on the A433 south of Tetbury, and only a short distance from Highgrove, the residence of the Prince of Wales.

Ann and Tony drove down the M4, leaving at junction 17, going through Malmesbury, and out on the B4040 to Eastern Grey, and taking a small road to the north to get through to Westonbirt.

Once at the Arboretum they parked, and quickly went to the main entrance, and checked no one was following them.

Not far inside, they disappeared off the path through over hanging branches, and were quickly concealed by officers in camouflage, who threw a type of poncho over them. The poncho was like a piece of long material with a hole in the middle. Having put it over their heads, the two sides were fastened leaving only the arms and head uncovered.

They were then lead over to an area used for plants, and into a safe area, where Mickey was waiting in a van with a large telescopic pole on top.

"Hi," Mickey said.
"Like the men of Sherwood," Tony said pointing to the poncho.
"Only we are the law," Mickey said.
"But he was the good guy, Robin Hood I mean," Ann added.
"No fighting today," Tony said, getting in quick before they could get into an argument.

"Where's Meldrum today?" Ann asked.

"He's working at home."

"Oh yes.... and how do you know?" Ann snapped.

"Let me show you," Mickey said picking up a mobile phone and dialling the number.

He spoke to Meldrum and hung up.

"See, he's at home. Nowhere near here."

"Can I try something?" Ann asked.

"What!"

Ann picked up the phone and spoke to the hotel.

"Fax 50 pages from my computer manual, the one in the ring binder to this number," she said giving Meldrum's fax number.

Once it was connected and the transmission was in hand, she handed the phone back to Mickey.

"Now see if he's at home."

Mickey dialled the number having muttered something about wasting time, and amateur detectives. The phone rang, and rang, there was no answer. Eventually he hung up.

"See," Ann said. "He's not there."

"He was, he must have just popped out," Mickey said not having a better explanation.

"Or on the loo," Tony added, hoping to defuse a developing argument.

"How?" Mickey asked, "could he fix his phone to go to any other place.

"Easy!" said Ann feeling superior. "A machine called a diverter. It answers your call and diverts out on a second line, direct to his mobile."

"Oh..." Mickey said thoughtfully, "and you think Meldrum has one of these diverters?"

"Yes."

Mickey had to admit it was a possibility, although discounted it as not really relevant for they would catch whoever it was.

Unknown to all of them Wendy had not stayed back at the hotel, but was also at the Arboretum. She had parked down the main road, and walked in across the fields.

Wendy knew the plan they had well, and had worked out how a gunman would behave. After Avebury, she thought it is obvious that when he spots them he will find the best point of escape, and take the shot from there.

She had worked out that a small gate, lead out of the Arboretum onto a track, and that a path lead from the gate to the area the trap was set.

The police had assumed that they would catch him in the bushes around the edge of the clearing, and had contingency plans involving both mounted officers and officers with motorcycles but they had to be kept well back so not to be seen.

Wendy had seen on TV, sometime back, a survival programme that showed how rabbits could be caught with snares, pieces of wire in a loop fixed to the ground. She had managed to get some strong wire from a hardware store, and a machine to crimp wire from a electronics firm. She had also obtained some large metal pegs from a camping shop.

She laid out several loops, attached to the large pegs on the ground, spaced unevenly along the path, and then knocked each of the pegs into the ground at a slight angle, with the top pointing towards the clearing. She covered up, as best she could, the wire and pegs with leaves and twigs.

It didn't look natural she thought, all the leaves and twigs on an otherwise clear path, but it was the best she could do.

She hid behind a bush, and got some string she had brought and a tie on parcel label.

Some time later there was a bang, and the dummy in the clearing fell over. Police whistles blew, and the chase began.

Wendy took cover as she heard someone running towards her, then there was a thump, as the persons foot was caught in one of the snares.

Wendy jumped out, before the gunman could think, and hit him over the head with the wooden mallet she used to put in the pegs. She then quickly tied up the gunman, and put his gun on the path ahead but out of his reach. Finally, she added the label which read 'Happy Un-Xmas, a little package for you' and underneath in smaller writing 'Place in a warm dry place, and store for many years.'

Having done this she quickly made her departure through the wood, and across a field back to her car.

The police were on the scene very quickly after Wendy had left and were more than a little surprised to find their prisoner, now conscious, tied up and pinned to the ground.

"You're under arrest.... you're nicked," Mickey said grabbing the tied up body. Turning him over he was surprised to find it was Meldrum,.

"Let me out you idiot," Meldrum said "they're getting away."
"Who?" Mickey said, now confused.
"The gunman, I found out what you were doing and thought I could help, but I got knocked out and tied up. Come on idiot untie me."
Mickey wasn't sure what to do, was Meldrum telling the truth, and if he wasn't who could have tied him up like this.

Mickey decided to be on the safe side, they would search the Arboretum, but keep Meldrum confined for the moment.

As Ann and Tony couldn't do anymore, they decided to go and visit the Cotswolds for the rest of the day. They visited Cirencester, Fairford, Lechlade which is the highest point boats can go on the River Thames. They went back to Fairford and through some small villages to get to Bibury, and after a walk around, and a good look at all the trout, through some more side roads turning right when they got to the A429, and up to Bourton on the Water. They visited the model village, which was unusual in that it was a model of the village they were in. They visited the gift shops, and bought postcards of the area, so they could show Wendy what it looked like.

There was a lot of other things to see at Bourton on the Water, but they wanted to see other places, so they visited Stow on the Wold, Moreton in the Marsh, ending up at Broadway on the A44 east of Evesham.
"Doesn't the family with Billy live near here?" Ann asked.
"Yes, it's... um Honeybourne," Tony said. "Can you see it on the map."

They found the village on the map, and within half an hour was in Honeybourne. They saw the thatched pub, and the church now converted into homes, and found the home of the Merryweather's in School Street.
"I wonder where John Pugh lived?" Ann asked.
"In part of what is now the thatched pub," Tony said.

They visited the Merryweather's, who were delighted to see them again, and they told them of the events at Westonbirt, the mysterious person who tied up Meldrum, and their trip up through the Cotswolds.
"It was the area John Pugh must have visited often when he was a younger man, and we found the spot his father had hidden his wealth then", Ann explained.
"Not that his father left him much, but having to find it, gave him the idea to set up the notebook."

That night as they drove back to the hotel, they discussed all that had happened, and all they had seen that day, and on arrival Wendy was interested to hear all about it.

Later when Wendy and Tony were alone, Tony said "Do you know, I just can't understand who could have tied up Meldrum and what did that funny note really mean?"
Wendy didn't answer as she sat closer, and he gave her a little cuddle.

Did he suspect, she wondered.

This book is part of a trilogy (3 books)

Another book, available now is:-

TO SEARCH AND PROSPER

Billy is special, Mandy and Bobby twins, their parents Alex and Sally and sister Cathy make up the Merryweather family. The story of this family, with amusing and moving parts would more than have kept you interested, without the friendly visiting Alien, reluctantly visiting earth.

You will meet the characters in this book several times, but of course see events from a different viewpoint. What happened when they were booking into the hotel?

The same clues are covered, on the way to the same treasure, but a different perspective may help.

Like this book you will find the pages keep turning with so much new happening all the time.

Available from:
Knowledge Base Publications Ltd
19 Penybryn, Mountain Ash,
Mid Glamorgan CF45 3TJ
OR Visa/Access orders on 0443-478754

PRICE: £9.95 (Post Free)
Or any good book shop. ISBN 1-898027-01-3

CHAPTER TWENTY SIX.

The following day they discussed what had happened, and looked at what to do next with the Treasure Trail, and it was the morning of the following day, Wednesday, and they were in Tony's flat.

Ann and Tony were looking at a map of the Cotswold area, and Wendy was working on the card index, when Mickey Jessett arrived.

"Any news on Meldrum?" Tony asked.
"Some, but we have a problem."
"What?" Ann asked.
"It was the person who tied him up, and moved the gun. They handled it you see. The question is how did it get there?"
"What?" Tony said in surprise. "He must have brought it."
"Well he says he was knocked out, and tied up, and that someone put it against his hands to get his finger prints."
"You don't believe that do you?" Tony asked.
Wendy was keeping quiet working on the card index.

"Well imagine you are a jury, and you hear his story. Came to help, was knocked over the head, tied up and left injured."
"Oh..." said Ann. "You think they would let him go?"
"So what will happen?" Tony asked.
"Oh... he'll stand trial."
"But if you don't think you will get a conviction," Ann said a little surprised.

"No you see, we know who tied him up."

"Who?" asked Tony.

"Me," Wendy said quietly, "I didn't want him to get away."

"Um..." Mickey said looking at Wendy, "we had your finger prints, and they were on both the gun and pegs."

"You don't think I shot at Tony?" Wendy said getting worried, and fearing being arrested again.

"No, you couldn't have been at the Nottingham or Avebury shootings, as you were in plain view when they happened, so you're in the clear."

"Oh... thank goodness," Wendy said, looking a bit more relieved.

"Going equipped, grievous bodily harm, assault, and a few other charges could always be arranged for your attack on Meldrum if you wanted," Mickey said with a smile.

"There isn't any chance of that is there?" Tony asked.

"No, we're sort of treating it as a citizens arrest, and as he was armed with a gun and you just happened to have a camping mallet in your hand, it was possibly reasonable force or self defence."

"Is that a guarantee?" Wendy asked, not realising the trouble she could have landed in.

"Yes this time. But please don't make a habit of it."

"What about the South Wales murder?" Tony asked. "Did Meldrum do that as well?"

"Probably. He had some of the papers taken from the solicitors office and your notebook hidden in his home."

"Can I have it back... the notebook I mean?" Tony asked.

"Eventually, but it's evidence for now."

"Will the contents of the notebook stay confidential?" Ann asked.

"It's not in Meldrum's interest to publish it, and we don't need to, so except for a few legal people it should be confidential."

"Isn't there anyway of getting it back now?" Ann asked.

"Don't worry," Tony said. "We still have the centre pages, so no one can find the treasure except us."

"Unless they're part of the alternative solution," Wendy added.

There was a silence, while everyone thought.
"There is a possibility someone else could find the treasure," Ann said, "and the only solution's to find it first."

"I can help," Mickey added, and then hesitantly looking at Ann, "if you want me too of course."
"Isn't it about time you two became friends," Tony said looking first at Ann and then at Mickey.
"Well yes," said Ann.
"I'm willing to," Mickey added.
"Okay. I have an idea. Why don't you two go on a trip to say Snowdonia, or the Norfolk Broads, and each try to understand the other."
"But wouldn't we just argue?" Mickey asked.
"No, you each except that the other has a point of view."
"Like you put up with vegetarians?" Ann asked.
"Yes, that's it."

Over the next six weeks, many places were revisited, various philosophies tried, and searches made. There were now three teams, Tony and Wendy, Ann and Mickey, and the Merryweather family.

Another obscure clue that had given them some difficulty read; Some homing pigeons set out from a castle. About five miles west of the original home and shop of a well-known Prime Minister.
It flew to the ghost of a comic menace.
Another left the old Friar Tuck script. Flew over a similar place, and on over a rapidly developing town. Pigeons like

the similar place, and a place similar to that, but not to the other.
Another left the eastern end of the druids home, and passed over something to go with a new lock, over north west point on the island and on.
Pigeons like familiar places like the city with two modern castles.
Or from Robins enemy's home over a north bridge to a familiar place.
Alternatively; from a start; from a west place north, to a child or comic place of religion.

They had visited Cardiff to solve another counting puzzle, which involved counting the number of carvings or statues on the wall between the castle entrance and the next building west. It said if there were more than 12 go left, less right, or 12 go straight on.

The most memorable of the visits over the last few weeks, had been only days ago when Tony and Wendy visited Ironbridge. There were a number of places to see there, including a tile museum, Coalbrookdale and the museum of iron, Coalport China Works, a Tar Tower, the Iron Bridge over 200 years old, and the most spectacular of all the Blist Hill Open Air Museum.

This is nothing like any museum you will have visited before but a whole village, with lots of shops, a print works, school, doctors surgery, mine, foundry, and much much more, all set up as it would have been in 1900.

Tony changed some of his money into old money at the bank, and was then able to buy things at 1900 prices in the pub, bakery, sweet shop, chemist and some other places.

Wendy was enthralled by the candlemaker, making candles in two colours, one for home and one for the mines. She bought some and was amazed to find that not only did the people dress and act according to the age, but the newspaper her candles were wrapped in was dated Saturday 21st April 1900. Wendy also liked the cobblers shop, plasterers shop and sweet shop, but did not like the slaughterhouse or butchers shop.

Tony found the bakery interesting, and the locksmiths, but spent longest watching the printing machines running in the print shop.

They had just left the squatters cottage and was aiming for the Mission Church, when they saw in the distance someone they thought that looked like Claire, with several children.

They walked as fast as they could, but gave up when they reached the inclined plane, without seeing any sign of them again.

The Hay Inclined Plane was two pairs of railway lines going up the side of a steep hill, special vessels known as Tub Boats were dragged up these, on wheeled cradles that ran over the iron rails. A steam engine was used. The device linked the River Severn at the bottom of the gorge with the Shropshire Canal at the top.

The notebook had just said visit Blists Hill Ironbridge, you will find it is a visit you will never forget.

A meeting was arranged at the hotel one Sunday afternoon, with all the teams, plus Claire and her grandfather. Quite a gathering. The plan was for a two day search on Monday and Tuesday. Ann and Mickey would search the

Cotswolds. The Merryweather's would continue their search of the English/Welsh border, and Wendy and Tony would follow up a number of possibilities in various places. Claire and her grandfather had also joined some of the searches and had been helping the Merryweather's, and Claire, her grandfather, and the two younger Merryweather's would be looking in some coastal locations.

The plans were all set, when Wendy had an idea pop into her head. "I know we are looking for a Dean Forest or wood or something similar, possibly on the English/Welsh border," Wendy had just said when she had the idea.
"I'll add another location to try out," she said.

Claire and her grandfather, went to the Merryweather's house at Honeybourne for the night, so as to get an early start the following morning.

Ann had taken a couple of days holiday, so was able to set off with Mickey to Oxford, and on to the Cotswolds.

So only Tony and Wendy had to work, but they would be able to set off early in the morning.

As Ann and Mickey drove to Oxford, they chatted occasionally about many things, for they had become good friends by now.
"If I tell you something, do you promise not to laugh," Mickey said hesitantly.
"What?"

"No. Promise first."

"I promise to try not to laugh, will that do?"

"I suppose it will have to."

"So," she asked impatiently.

"Well, this may sound silly for a policeman, but... um... I believe that behaviour is effected by diet."

"You mean bad food makes bad people," Ann said trying not to laugh.

"You promised," Mickey said looking a little hurt. "Yes there is evidence to prove some foods effect children, cut out the foods and problem children become normal."

"Are you serious..... I thought you were in favour of hanging and all that."

"No that's just an act. You imagine how I would be treated in the force if I went around saying, joy riders had just had too many baked beans."

"Doesn't that make you um.... um a um....."

"Hypocrite," Mickey interrupted. "Yes, but what can I do?"

"What do you want to do?"

"I can't do it but... sort of set up a home for children to come to, and um.. sort of work out what they can eat, and monitor their behaviour."

"A home or a prison?"

"It would have to be secure. But it would be run as a home."

"So why don't you do it?"

"Money."

"That's a cop out, you could raise money if you wanted too."

"Cowardice, I suppose then. There would be opposition from all sides."

"So!"

"So, um... I don't know."

They discussed the idea, and the more Ann heard the more she thought it would be worth trying. Anything that would stop children turning into problems, or keep children with problems from having to end up as convicts, had to be worth looking at.

"You have my support," Ann said eventually. "I will help you set up a charity to fund it."
"I would have to give up my police career."
"So!"
"How would I live until I get it going... if I did?"
"Be positive.... you get your friends to help. You know how much Tony likes children he would help."
"Would he?"
"Yes... tomorrow night we will put it to the treasure hunters, you will see they will all be behind you."

"I hope so," Mickey said not sure if he was yet ready to openly admit what many police officers have discussed in private for years.
"You, a man or a mouse?" Ann asked squeezing his hand.
"If only I had your confidence," he said with a smile.

CHAPTER TWENTY SEVEN.

The following day they all proceeded as planned. With four groups out a lot of ground was to be covered. A lot of the ground covered had been covered before, and they now all knew their way around the country, and had a good idea of where John Pugh had come from, had spent his youth, had worked, spent his holidays, and his retirement.

They had all gained from the search. In knowledge of the country, in interests, and most of all in friendships. It no longer mattered if the treasure was found or not, and Ann and Wendy had agreed that in many ways it would be a bad thing, in that the group might fall apart, if they did not have a common purpose.

Tuesday, likewise, the teams were out, checking facts, following up possibilities, and hoping the next possible solution would lead to the treasure. As the evening approached they collected together in a small hotel in Malvern, just over 40 miles from Birmingham. Claire's team were the first to arrive, followed by the rest of the Merryweather's, and then Ann and Mickey.

They had all enjoyed the two days out, but were no nearer the treasure. Ann and Mickey had just started to explain the idea of a children's centre, along the lines they had discussed over the previous few days, when Tony and Wendy arrived. As Tony and Wendy seemed excited by what they had heard, they continued their presentation.
"Well what do you think?" Mickey said. "Would you all support me, I mean us," he looked at Ann for support.
"Of course they will, won't you?"

Everyone without exception agreed it was a good idea. Feeling more confident Mickey turned to Ann.
"Ann, we have become great friends, and you have already said how much you would like to work with me. How about becoming Mrs Jessett?"

Ann looked at Tony, what should she say. She liked both Mickey and Tony. In fact over the last few days she had realised she probably had a lot more in common with Mickey. But would it be letting Tony down. Did he expect her to wait for him some day.
"Go on, say yes," Tony said encouraging her.
"Yes," Ann said, throwing her arms around Mickey.
Tony stepped forward, "and I have a little something to get your venture off to a flying start," he handed Ann an envelope.
"A cheque. Where did you get all this money from?" Ann asked in embarrassment. "It's an absolute fortune."
Seeing Mickey looking at him, he pretended to be worried.
"Honest Officer, it's mine."
They all laughed.
Wendy interrupted, "it's the treasure, we found it this morning. What's more there is more in the alternative treasure if we can find it."
"But it's yours," Ann said, not knowing whether to accept it or not.
"No, Mickey told me of his plans some time ago. I mean the charity thing. I have only one question."
Everyone looked.
"What?" Mickey asked.
"How do I apply for the chef's job?"
"You've got it, but on half the salary you get now," Ann quickly replied.
"Okay... One more question."
"What?" Ann asked, wondering what surprise lay in store.
"If Wendy agrees, can we make it a double wedding?"

APPENDIX ONE.

TREASURE TRAIL - INSTRUCTIONS

You will know that besides being a book you can read and hopefully enjoy, this book also contains two Treasure Trails. It is part of a series of four books, three of which lead to the treasure. There are also four fun solutions, allowing certificates to be collected.

THE TREASURE TRAIL:- A story of an inherited notebook, giving clues to a hidden fortune. It is in part a detective story, with a small team of main characters. Some romance and comedy is included. The pace of the book is very fast. There is a murder, attempted murder, and a number of other happenings which will keep the pages turning. (Published 1993) ISBN 1-898027-00-5 £14.95 Hardback, 244 pages, 234 x 156mm.
TO SEARCH AND PROSPER:- This story tells the Treasure Trail from a totally different viewpoint, although the family this book is based on meet the people in the other book several times. It is based on a family, and a visiting alien (from outer space). They have a number of adventures along the way. It is a different story amusing and moving in places. (Published 1993) £9.95
ISBN 1-898027-01-3 Hardback, 160 pages, 234 x 156mm.
FAME OR FORTUNE:- This story starts three years after the end of "The Treasure Trail". The same characters are now involved in totally different situations. One is a wealthy writer unknown to the others, several now run a detective agency. You will also see the people you met in "To Search and Prosper", all now also three years older. While attempting to solve a variety of mysteries, and as they travel around remember parts of the treasure trail solution. Depending on what has happened with the Treasure Trail this could help reveal the original or

alternate solutions. (To be published 1995)
ISBN 1-898027-02-1 £14.95 Hardback 234 x 156mm
<u>RAINBOWS END</u>:- A children's book, illustrated throughout by children, with all the profit from this book going to children's charities. It will provide a series of clues to look for while accompanying other members of the family on the Treasure Trail. Simple form to fill in and mail to get a certificate. The story is of a boy and girl and two garden gnomes, who come to life having been hit by a firework, and they hear of little people and the pot of gold at the end of the rainbow. The rest you may be able to guess. (To be published for Christmas 1993)
ISBN 1-898027-03-X

FUN SOLUTIONS.

Each book in addition to the treasure trail, has an additional fun solution, which is far simpler, and allows you to get, with a single trip, all the information needed to get a certificate. There are four certificates to collect.

THE TREASURE.

The Treasure starts at £6,000 when the first book comes out, and increases with 10% of the cover price of all books sold, with the exception of Rainbows End.

Until the Treasure reaches £15,000, or is found, all goes into the primary or main treasure. Between £15,000 and £30,000 the treasure slowly moves into two amounts, so that at £30,000, £25,000 is in the main chest and £5,000 in the second or alternate. From this point on all new treasure generated from sales is split equally between the two. In theory therefore, as we expect it to take two or three years to solve the puzzle, (but of course you may do it faster), the primary treasure will be £20,000 more than the secondary.

Once the primary treasure has been found all new treasure goes into the secondary treasure chest. This will cause it to grow rapidly.

The search for the secondary treasure cannot officially start until the primary treasure has been found. Of course there is no reason why you should not have a head start. Further details on the second location is in Appendix Two.

All the information you need to solve the location of the two treasures, is contained in both of the first two books in the sequence, although they concentrate on hunting for the primary treasure. An exact description of the last few miles to the treasure is explained in both cases, in a coded section, and you are given information on how to decode the section relevant to the primary treasure, in such detail that anyone can do it.

WHAT IS AT THE LOCATION.

At the primary location, there is a container, sitting on the surface, it may be camouflaged. No digging or damage needs to be done. The container has in it a piece of paper written in the same code as in the coded section telling you how to get your reward. It is important to stress that no digging or damage or access to private property is necessary.

The secondary location has nothing at it, there is a separate section following that explains the secondary treasure hunt in more detail.

CAN I GET HELP?

You can band together with others, form large groups or solve it on your own. You will not be surprised to find that the author will not provide any help whatsoever. A club service is provided, details later, which you can use or not. It will provide information annually on the size of the treasure, and information on clues that have changed, if for example, roads change or developments take place.

WHERE IS IT NOT?

It is not:-

- Buried
- On Private Property
- Near any building or historical site
- Near the authors home, or anywhere he has lived or worked
- Outside the mainland of England and Wales
- In or around Honeybourne
- In or around Avebury.

The solutions to any part of this is not kept at the home of the author, or the publishers premises.

THE OBJECTS OF THIS QUEST.

To many people it will be the chance to try their brain against everyone else, or the treasure itself that will attract them, but the main objective of this project is to encourage people to visit other parts of Britain, and enjoy everything around them. If it fosters new interests so much the better. Everyone who takes part will benefit, will see and enjoy new places and interests, and even if you don't find the treasure it should be an experience you will never forget.

WHAT ELSE WOULD IT COST YOU.

There are a few places you have to pay to enter, details on these and their opening hours are listed in Appendix Nine. In theory you don't need to spend anything else, although the cost of travelling about can be quite expensive. This can be reduced by planning your trips so as to combine these visits with other events, or several of these places together. You do not need to visit every place mentioned in the book. It is up to you to decide where to visit. Remember books and maps can also often prove helpful.

The book referred to as the 'green brick', can be obtained from Family History Club, 19 Penybryn, Mountain Ash, Mid Glamorgan CF45 3TJ. Priced £18.95 plus £2.85 post and packing (paperback), or £28.95 plus £2.85 post and packing (hardback). Orders can be placed over the telephone against a Visa or Access card on 0443-475900. You will of course realise you do not have to buy this book, you could look at it in a library, or using the same techniques use anything else you could find written by the same author, or probably any other, although you may need a little more practise.

A SLIGHT WARNING OR TWO.

Removal of the solution, although allowing the treasure to grow will put you at a risk of losing it. If we find it has gone, it will be replaced. So with the initial treasure do not sit on your claim. There is no prize for coming in second.

With the initial solution you need to decode it using the same code as the final solution (the coded section in Chapter Fifteen). Do not take any notice of anything written in English as it is meant for anyone stumbling across it by accident.

COPYRIGHT.

The copyright of the text in this and other books in the series belongs to the author, who may authorise other editions, or serialisation if he wishes, but in all cases there will be a contribution towards the treasure. The solutions to the coded sections are also copyright, as they exist in their decoded form.

COMMON SENSE.

Common sense may help you. The concept is that an elderly man with a bad heart hid this treasure. He would not have been able to climb cliffs, or get anywhere else too way out. He would also not have put the treasure where it would likely to be discovered by accident or be destroyed by development. Common sense will tell you, that to have all the books in the series will give you an advantage. Please remember that you do not need to dig any holes or do any damage.

MAILING LIST.

If you want to be kept informed of other books by the Author, or other Treasure Trail news then please either see the Club information or send in your name and address and ask to be added to the mailing list.

CHANGES IN THE RULES.

The Author reserves the right to change the rules of this game, if necessary, and should one or both of the treasures not be eventually found to donate all the proceeds from these to charities. He must however, give three years notice of his intention to do this.

APPENDIX TWO.

THE SECONDARY LOCATION.

With a Treasure Trail, there is a problem. Do you make it so hard no one will find it, or do you devise it in such a way that someone is likely to find it.

If you make it too easy, someone will find it, and may do so quickly, and therefore there is no future or motivation for others.

Our solution has been to split the treasure into two pots, the secondary pot growing once the primary one has reached a set size or been found.

Of course you may say, the problem still exists with the secondary treasure, or someone could discover it before the first pot had been found.

To overcome all these problems we have devised a few rules to this game.

1. There is less help in the text, so in theory the second solution is harder to solve.
2. There is less in the motivation as it does not have a value to start, and will always be smaller than the primary one, until the first is found. It will then grow very fast.
3. Officially the hunt for the alternative solution does not start until the primary treasure is found.
4. The solution to the secondary or alternate solution is not a physical item but two grid references,

ALTERNATIVE SOLUTION.

This coded section gives you the detailed description of between 20 and 30 miles, all on roads, mainly major roads. From this section you obtain two ordnance survey grid references (see instructions). The initial solution should be completed first, but it's always worth keeping your eyes open.

```
ICXPPXAXCGMZKYZIGIWXOMCAMZCJNKMNCBNLVQRO
GCBGRWFQWOFNLCBNINLWCNBGINDCNINFZGWNLWRL
BVVZMNLCXQWODQWOICVQRMQWCNKUYZGQGOINMZBD
FRMCVLNRMCFNGZBFNIQGGONMIFICNBQWOBUQWEIL
IBQWFZGNMXGWMZRNASCVLCNNONBZQWMIBGENMZUO
ICNBIQRGBFQWOJRNJGCBGGXWWANBGGMZRMCGGYWD
ZBGYWMZWAXNYNIRNFMNIGRNNMZIUNBWYFWGQWOIL
NMRNOYQWCJZAWOIQSRMWPIMCXGCJXZZNWFMUIVNO
OXGMZVZDQWBFCNIWANBGGZKUMQWOFXINGMZZGXNL
LNXIVCINXXMUNGYCGDWVZXNBBGWKVWYXURZIIWND
CFKJRIIWSWWYXCGZXNDFMCORQUFAJWMZZMFXQGIO
DWMPIQWORWWDQWOXUQWINBGBWURCBGXNBGINWIND
VNGCJNVZRMMWAWCFWGGXMCNFNBBFNIGNGMBGWAZO
BUZNMNNGMZVNGCXUZPMZNYUMONLZXCQWMXNWUGWD
ZBRXPMGXGWZBJZGNCBGRZLUMFNCBXGRZNBQWMWGO
NRQWNRZFZXGQOFNRRZXMWIWNWBFMZNXWWONLCFQD
GMZYAMZWGMNNNXNLXMGCGBIQWIUQINWKANGNGXBO
WDGGMNJWFFNGIZBZWAMNCUMZVGGCRMMZPMZNNYUL
UQWOXCGNJNLVXNVZCXBUNDGGKINGQWIWUMZWNACD
NKFWGRNIWYWOYZARNNMQCFRWWWGXRMJXCOKDVVCL
VVVQFGYNZBNKAXRMNBGNDWIFNMWGLCNVANLZMZWD
CXYGWDRWGMCWGCZNXZUCNBNINIGNGMBGAIZWWYQO
QWDDWGCXRVXCMIQIFNBGNGCVNGQWOIRMCWDVZJCL
MZGGWDWACXGGVZXNDGJWFIGCWUNLWUMZWYNIKRNO
```

(explained later), so more than one person can solve it.

5. There is a twelve month delay, to allow others to solve it before a further sheet is given to those finding the solution which will take someone with less thought, to the hidden treasure.

NOW IN DETAIL.

To get the secondary treasure, which you will appreciate could climb to be far larger than the first, you use many of the same clues, and logic as the first. Therefore we assume the old man had some common practices or ideas. (This is a hint).

The coded section, which you don't get any help to crack, is far more difficult, but once you have cracked it, can be of enormous help covering a distance of over 20 miles. You need to identify two points on a map, giving a grid reference for each one. Grid references are explained in Appendix Six. They comprise of two letters and six numbers.

Having solved the puzzle and found the two points, you write them down and remember to add your name and address. Draw a red box around the references and send them, to the author, or the address given in the annual report of the club. As the address in the annual report is the most up to date it may be the best to use. Enclose £5.

You will then within a month, either receive back your sheet, telling you your guess is not correct, or if correct you will receive your £5 back with the date you will get the final instructions.

If you are the first to send in the correct grid references,

ALTERNATIVE SOLUTION contd.

NXRMCWWDCNNBGBUFVVCDPVCDWQWIBGMQGIWGOGZL
BGNRAAWNNZYYZXRVQWOMNBXIQWOXWNNXJGBUNVZD
GMZNANZWGCMWMZXGMNWAQIPMBGRNRVGCYYNZBXNO
DWGUXRICQGFNMZMINIGCLWJNWOPMNNXQQWOXZBGD
NMZMGBGMNGZIAWICXNGCBDUMZAACMNFBUQWWINHL
NQMZBGVCXMWZGMWFZRINGFNINBGMGNSNWINBZRCD
FXAZBGNPCGKFUMZXWMGQXBFCNBGNJWGXZIKIFVWL
DWGUXRICNKRMMZICNHWGCFWIDWMPMNBDDQWOVVZD
FNIZRXMWZGGMZUMDNMNBWICMWZWURCICGXXUMZGL
WUXNNBNIBGMNRCFOQWNIICONRWXWCBGGWXDMWZMO
XMZINGFQIGXXMWZBGWNNNLZGCGQVWXVCNBGMINGL
MWYWZAZMQWWIZGOXWBZDGGXWGNSNRMBGICQWWKSO
GQAXRNICNIVCGIWANBGMQMMCXZVMZRNGNAIWWXID
CNBGIIWBGQXZBFZNBGZNINARNBDMWXNAXNBZYZFL
GGGWMNZRMCXRNIXXCRRRNJMCIQCMBGWOINZDGNBO
NACAYUWGFIACMWNWNFNZGZIDXXNBGNIWAJZGMCGL
CVNIYQNNXGWOWAMZGMWDRZWNRRFNFDMCVWWVXZYO
LCBQWWRWGNXNVZJOVVCXGINLWOGMNDQWICUYWNGL
LWFXMZINFQIGMWZGWOXNXMZQWZGFLZUMNRWFNXRD
BGXZRWXNBGFNPFRNFFCINMGZNLWRQWCBXNOFXMOO
BGBGZWWAXNMCIBXDOCDCRMCFMZRNBGQXNNXQYBFL
RNWGQCBUWRVUGGNVNBZVMWGFNBWJNLGINAWRQEJO
GNVRRDWFNBRMCGCZYNBGVRRZRFNBGNZRONBNVRRL
TWJDPSIGBVEKRHMYXNQOACFZUL

A=32.
B=83

then the date will be in 12 months time or twelve months from the date the first treasure is found. If others have found it before you it will be 12 months from the first one to find the points. Therefore on a set date everyone who has by that time worked out the solution will be given the final sheets together. If you come across the points after they have started you will be given the information straight away.

The £5 charge is to eliminate us being buried in random entries. The final section on the sheet will not require any more visits, or decoding, and will stay with the Ordnance Survey map of the point found or one in any direction. So once you have found the point it may be worth familiarising yourself with the surrounding area.

If you find the location you should consider which is the best point to declare you know it. The longer you wait, the higher the prize, but the more competition you will have on the final solution.

OTHER SOLUTIONS.

You will find the basic story and clues can give a number of starting points. Therefore by creating further coded sections other treasure hunts are possible. See Club information on development in this area.

FUN SOLUTION.

A simpler solution is offered as a fun solution. This does not require any decoding and is a separate puzzle. It does not lead to any treasure, but you can get a certificate. See Appendix Three.

The Author reserves the right to change the rules of this game. See Appendix One.

APPENDIX THREE

THE FUN SOLUTION.

INTRODUCTION.

A simpler puzzle, not leading to any treasure is explained in this section. There is no coded section and most if not all the basic information is enclosed in this book. So only one visit is necessary.

If you solve it, and are a member of the club, detailed in appendix four, then you can get a certificate to show what a genius you are. If you are not a member of the club you can apply for a certificate, but it costs you £3 per application, so no guessing.

To apply, write your name and address on a sheet of paper, followed by "FUN SOLUTION 1", and then the solution. If you are not a club member enclose your cheque made out to Keith Park (address in Appendix Four).

Each of the four books has a different fun solution, so there are four certificates to collect.

WHAT YOU HAVE TO SOLVE FOR THIS BOOK

Identify where John Pugh lived when he was young, went on holiday and retired to. This gives you three points.

Draw lines on a map to form a triangle. Measure half way along each line, and draw a line to the opposite point of the triangle.

You now have a small triangle which includes a bit of motorway. Within your small triangle, or very near it, depending on your map and drawing, is a place you might go to see something which could have been fun at a place said to be near Northampton.

Go from this place north until you get to the junction of two main roads, at a place that reminds you of a battle. Go north east, past a place featured in this book, to a town beginning with a T, and south to a town with an Abbey.

Follow a road to the east towards a town beginning with a C. Cross a railway line by a pub, and continue until you get to a cross roads. Take the road south until you get to another crossroads, and go east to a village beginning with a P.

This you will find is a little visited yet interesting place, it has an earth works castle, many historic houses, one of only three churches with a tower and spire, (probably the only one totally separate). This village has many times played an important part in many ways, from being the home of Edward Hyde, who was the head of the British Government in Exile when Cromwell took over. Later it was the home of various parts of the Maskelyne family, prominent in the East India Company, and Nevil Maskelyne the Astronomer Royal, who was responsible for the longitude and latitude lines around the globe. He is buried in the church yard.

If you visit the church, notice the Tythe Barn nearby.

A couple of miles to the south is the point, where it is said in 1819, the last public hanging took place in Britain.

Your task is to discover what in the days of toll roads, the cost of taking a coach and four horses through Collins Lane

Gate would have been. The answer is in shillings and pence. (There were 12 pence in a shilling).

You will find a trip down Station Road may help.

APPENDIX FOUR.

TREASURE TRAIL CLUB.

This is an optional club you can join, with very special, and very limited services to members. There is no necessity to join, and no guaranteed advantage to you. Read the description of services below and decide if it is for you. You do not need to join the club to claim the treasure.

SERVICES.

ANNUAL REPORT:- The main service is an annual report, which updates you on the size of the treasure, and any facts that have changed since the origination of the book text. This is always possible when new developments, or changes can occur.

FINDERS REPORT 1:- When the initial treasure is found, members will be sent a description of how the solution worked, and the location of the initial treasure. A description of the container and other instructions may also be given. This will be sent out between 3 and 6 months after it is found.

FINDERS REPORT 2:- Like Finders Report 1 this will be sent out after the second treasure is found, not after the points are discovered.

FUN SOLUTION CERTIFICATES:- Club members solving any of the four fun solutions, can submit and receive their certificates at no cost. This service is provided within the annual membership cost.

OTHER TREASURE HUNTS:- The Club may also run additional fun solutions, or treasure hunts. All members will be kept informed of this and other books coming out by the same Author.

CHECKING SERVICE:- There are a limited number of solutions to clues, which can be checked. They are numbered at the end of this section. This is not designed to eliminate your need to do research, but to allow you to check you have the right solution if you get to the final route and it does not work out. We do not encourage guessing. To use it (and this is only open to club members), write your name and address and the club number and your solution on a sheet and send it in together with a £10 checking fee. Only one item may be checked at a time. No other solutions can be checked. You will receive back your solution marked with a tick if it is what we were looking for, and a cross if it is wrong, or a question mark if it is a correct answer or possibility, but not what we were expecting. No discussion on these items will be entered into. The high checking fee is intended to make this a last resort, not an option to use instead of doing the research yourself.

SITE CHECKING:- If you feel you have found the place where the treasure was, or should have been, and it was not there, then work out the grid reference of the position and send it in together with your name and address, and a £25 checking fee. We will then check that it is still on site, and within a month confirm to you that a check has been made. No discussions will be entered into. The cost eliminates this being used as a random checking operation. A physical check will only be made if the position you give is within half a mile of the actual position. We will not tell you if it is the correct or incorrect solution.

In any event there will be a check occasionally that it is still where we left it.

CODED SECTION:- Following the instructions in this book, anyone can decode the initial solution. Therefore the only reason anyone would, in theory, need help is if they are too lazy to work it out. Three levels of help are available.

A. COUNTS. Both the coded section and the section of the book referred to are analysed, and counts of each letter occurring in each case is provided sorted in order so the most used is at the top in both cases. No explanation beyond this is provided. Cost £30.

B. UNCODING. The counts previously, the initial decode options, and full decode keys are provided. All you have to do is to transfer it letter for letter. Cost £65.

C. FULL DECODING. The same as B, plus extra explanation, plus the full decoded text. Cost £95.

You should not need to use this service. It is provided simply for those who would otherwise employ someone else to do it for them. These solutions are provided on condition that they are copyright, and kept confidential.

No decoding service is available for the alternative solution, as solving this is a major part of the puzzle. The concept being that decoding the initial one will help you.

HOW TO JOIN THE CLUB

The cost of the annual report and financial report are included in the annual membership fee. The other services are optional and directions for use are detailed above.

To join send in your request to join and a £5 joining fee.

You will be sent a standing order which you sign and return. This is for £5 per annum. You may cancel your membership and the standing order at any time.

All cheques should be made payable to the author, Mr Keith Park, who will personally run the checking services. The fee is expected to cover the reports, and checking fees, and will possibly allow him to recover the £6,000 initial treasure he had to provide. His contract prohibits him from providing any other help to you.

LIST OF CHECKING CLUES:

No.	Clue	Answer	
1.	National Pinetum.		
	Height of Tree	__________	metres.
2.	Port well is nearest	__________	(number).
3.	Bentley. Colour of Cat	__________	(colour).
4.	Number of sphinx	__________	(number).
5.	Number of octagons	__________	(number).
6.	Date of Early Driving Licences	__________	(year).
7.	Number of bird paintings	__________	(number).
8.	Sheffield. Left/right/ahead	__________	(direction)
9.	Peterborough. Left/right/ahead	__________	(direction)
10.	David had a	__________	(item).
11.	Bristol. Bridge is left/right	__________	(direction)
12.	Exeter. Left/right	__________	(direction)
13.	Nottingham. Original text for Friar Tuck now	__________	(place).
14.	? Town in clock name	__________	(place).
15.	Northampton. Left/right	__________	(direction)

This you will appreciate is not a full list of clues. There are many more. Only these above can be checked.

You don't need to join the club to claim the treasure.

APPENDIX FIVE.

LOCAL TREASURE TRAIL CLUBS

People for various reasons, have much more leisure time than they used to have. This together with the desire people have to go somewhere with a purpose, means that special Treasure Trail Clubs would appeal to a lot of people.

A Club would do several things. It would organise local Treasure Hunts, initially for it's own members, but also for visiting clubs. It would likewise arrange for its members to take part in local treasure trails either individually or in teams, at events organised by other Treasure Trail Clubs. People would also work together within a club, to solve puzzles as part of the major Treasure Trail project. Events put on locally would also raise money for charity.

It would therefore encourage tourism, helping employment in your area, and encourage people to visit other areas.

It would raise money for charity, and make people's lives more enjoyable.

Sponsorship should be available locally from hotels, and others including councils who will benefit from the increased tourism.

Why not give it a go, either on your own or get a committee together, and let us know what you are doing, so we can help clubs to work together.

Co-ordination will be headed by:-
Federation of Treasure Trail Clubs
c/o Knowledge Base Publications Ltd, 19 Penybryn,
Mountain Ash, Mid Glamorgan CF45 3TJ.

APPENDIX SIX.

USEFUL SKILLS.

GRID REFERENCES:

Ordnance survey and possibly some other maps contain lines up, down and across. These are all numbered.

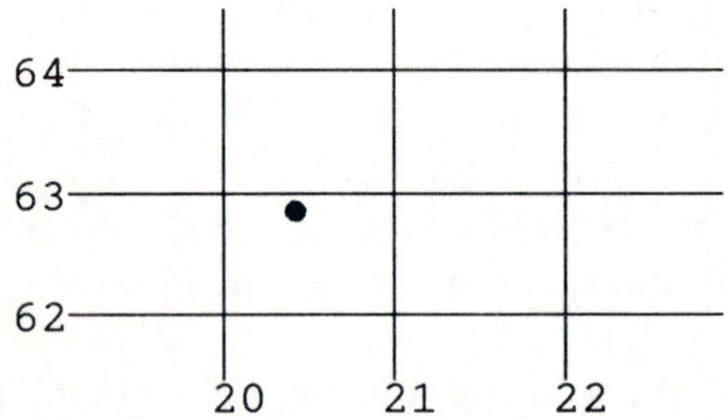

A grid reference is made up of two letters this relates to the large squares or sections of the map. These are indicated on the edge of the map.

To this you add three digits. Two, being taken directly from the bottom of the map so in the case above (20). You then estimate the number of tenths of the square so in the case above it is half way or five tenths. You therefore have (205).

Likewise you do the same up the side to get (629).
The full reference in this case if it was in area TQ, would be TQ 205 629.

This is a unique position. All you have to remember is that you use the bottom before the side. I remember this by saying you go along the passage and then up the stairs.

COMPASS DIRECTIONS:

There are four main points to the compass, North, South, East and West.

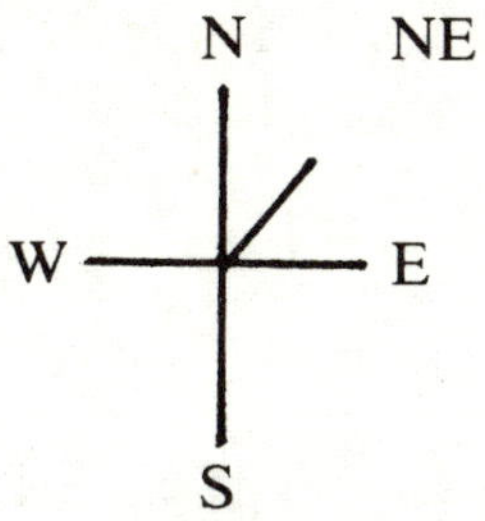

The division between North and East is North East, and half way between North and North East is North North East.

A compass divides this into 360 degrees, so East is at 90 degrees, South at 180 degrees and West at 270 degrees.

You can estimate the position of the compass from your position using the sun. As it rises in the East and sets in the West (or towards that way), you can deduce that halfway between sunrise and sunset it will be in the South. A bit before it will be towards South South East, and a bit after towards South South West.

Looking at the sun at this point is facing South, and putting your arms out your left arm points to 90 degrees (or East), and your right arm to 270 degrees (or West). You can estimate very roughly from this, any position without buying a compass. The method is good enough for this project.

If you want to find it more accurately for your own interest, and do not have a compass you can do it with a watch. You can look this up in a survivors guide or similar. We have an accurate compass.

GETTING ORGANISED:

You can take any chapter in any sequence, your search does not have to be in the order of the book. Work out all the places you want to go and putting together a plan could save you both time and cost. You need to be organised. You also need to keep your eyes open. You cannot use a map to find the final solution, as not all these features are shown on the map.

MAPS GENERALLY:

Map projections vary slightly, this may in part be due to the projection and scale. The earth being curved, and a map flat, corrections need to be made. This should not concern you except that if you were to draw shapes with lines they may change factionally from one map to another. Drawing lines from a town to a town, may vary slightly depending on the point in each town taken. I am not saying this effects you in anyway, and in any event, if it did, you may consider it to be insignificant.

APPENDIX SEVEN.

COULD YOU BE, OR ARE YOU AN AUTHOR

I hope that you enjoy reading this book as much as I enjoyed writing it. I visited most of the places featured, and have tried to give you the opportunity while hunting for the treasure to visit many interesting parts of Britain.

Perhaps you could write a book. This is my first fiction book and it did not turn out as difficult a task as I had expected. The characters, scenes, and events have come very much to life in my head, but for those interested in writing, perhaps the following few notes may explain how the books were written, and some of the decisions, as an author, I had to make.

I started with a very brief outline plot. I then produced in a flip up photo album a lot of cards. On the right of the album were plot units, or parts of the story. The card was divided up into location, situation or problem, dramatic high spot or emotion, and the back had information on the characters in that unit, their emotional drive and some additional notes. These plot units followed the sequence of the plot, and eventually having extended the plot, they were numbered so that one or more made up a chapter. The other side of the album had cards dealing with places, clues and puzzles. Next I created an A4 sheet on each character. Their age, description, education, work history, likes and dislikes, and much more so that each became a person.

The people within these were added to the plot units. In the case of this book of course a lot of visits were necessary and other research, and the plot units and other cards are all cross indexed.

Next it was decision time. Was I going to explain in detail the main characters. I decided not; so you could use your pictures, and identify better with a character. I also decided not to define the cars. Wendy in my view had a battered blue metro, Ann a bright white new BMW, and Tony a rather special Ford, but of course as this does not appear in the book, they drive what you see in your mind.

Next the viewpoint. First person, told form the position of a single character, or some other. The view point I have chosen is the restricted third person. You see and experience things for all of the main characters, but you can't see the thoughts of lesser characters. You are also only in one place, and have one viewpoint at a time. If you want to see the effect of this look at the hotel booking in sequence in chapter 16 of this book and chapter 5 of 'To Search and Prosper'. In this book you see it from Wendy's viewpoint, or rather an object next to Wendy, while in the other book you see it from the Merryweather's situation. There are other examples as the plots of these two books cross over.

The next decision was the balance between dialogue and description. I have chosen to use a lot of dialogue, which makes the story appear to go faster, at the expense of description. Although in places there is quite a lot of description. This type of work is therefore often termed popular fiction as opposed to literary fiction which has more descriptions. Like a radio play, I hope you find the pictures that form in your mind are far clearer than anything I could have defined.

There were of course many other decisions, the type of

language. Whether to have X rated scenes. How strong or weak to make various characters, and the emotions I wanted to stir. Where to leave a scene, and what options I can safely leave in the mind of readers as actions at the points when we leave.

If you enjoyed this book, then I hope you will be encouraged to write your own, and give other people pleasure. If you didn't, then of course you will know you can do better.

Knowledge Base Publications Ltd would be interested to know what you have or could write. Remember whatever anyone tells you, publishers need authors as much as authors need publishers.

APPENDIX EIGHT.

EXTRACTS OF:

TO SEARCH AND PROSPER

By KEITH PARK

Billy is special, Mandy and Bobby twins, their parents Alex and Sally and sister Cathy make up the Merryweather family. The story of this family, with amusing and moving parts would more than have kept you interested, without the friendly visiting Alien, reluctantly visiting earth.

The same clues as 'The Treasure Trail' although experienced with a different perspective and totally different story.

CHAPTER ONE.

THE BRIEFING.

Sex, sex, sex, nothing but sex. That's all these humans seem interested in thought Dagonite 763, as it listened to another lecture on earth. Why did he have to attend anyway, after all he was only number three in the tree biology unit. Perhaps I should mention there were only three in this unit.

"Earth, you can see from our last reconnaissance mission in 1873, is a primitive place," said the tutor, "people travel in primitive carts pulled by semi-trained animals, usually horses."
Boring, boring, boring thought 763. A cup of pine needle tea would suit me now.

He listened to the rest of the presentation, about heavy steam driven machines on metal rails, called trains, and about many other things, but not much was sinking in. After all why did it matter what these earthlings did.
"763," the tutor shouted, "tell us what you know about Great Britain.
"Um.. a ship. Big, ugly, metal with poles and engines."
"No, the country."
"Oh... it's on the um, north half of the planet, and an island I think."
"Yes, and what is special about it?"
"Has several interesting collections of trees, arboretums, pinetums and the like."
"No. It is the centre of an empire, which covers many parts of the world."
"Oh," 763 said settling back down into thinking of other

things.

"Our mission," said the tutor, "is to put one lone explorer on to Great Britain, somewhere near the middle. Their task will be to update us with any other developments since the last visit. There probably won't be any, and there is a biology reason as well."

763 had heard all about earth, it was the place his people had escaped from many thousands of years ago. He had heard of dinosaurs, or primitive people, and terrible weather conditions or ice periods lasting thousands of years. Some descendants of his ancestors still lived on earth, but had mutated. They were known as penguins by the earthlings, other branches had turned into whales and seals.

Of course, by looking at 763, you would not have recognised much similarity except with the penguin. He stands 2'9" or about a metre tall, has a penguin like body, no arms or legs, a head the size and shape of a large ball, with two large eyes towards the top. Slightly above the position humans would have ears, 763 had his, well everything. They looked like two hands with four fingers on each, but they were also ears, and transmitters and receivers for telepathic energy. Noises could also be generated and transmitted from these, and focused in any direction. Having no arms or legs, 763 like all the Dagonites got around by bouncing. Dagonites were various colours, but 763 is mainly pink.

"That's it," the tutor said, "except for 763, report to the Admirals quarters."
Oops, 763 thought, now I'm in trouble, but what have I done?

A few minutes later, both his little hearts beating so loud that it made him vibrate, he entered the Admirals quarters. Past the armed guards, and stood quite still now, not knowing what he had done.
"763," the Admirals assistant said, "you have been selected for the earth mission."
"No not me," 763 replied, after all why should it be him.
"Yes you, here is your briefing pack and a beacon so we can find you again." 763 was handed a file of paper and a device on a string that looked like a large black plastic stop watch.
"The beacon will tell you the time, date, elapsed time, and can be used to transmit to us twice," the Admirals assistant explained. "Twice only remember, and on two dates only. Otherwise you stay there forever."
"Why me?" 763 asked, not wanting to be chosen for the mission.
"Quite frankly, and I shouldn't probably tell you this, we don't think the beacon will work."
"So I might not be picked up?"
"That's it, and the computer says your the least valuable member of the crew."

He was going to be dumped on a primitive planet, probably with no chance of escaping, reluctantly he left.
"Read the section on things that might eat you," the Admirals assistant cried as he left, "and don't get wet."

I'm not stupid, he thought, I know not to get wet.

You will know this is one of two initial books leading to treasure. A third book in this series will be available for somewhen in 1995.

It will be called:-

FAME OR FORTUNE

This book will start three years after the end of this one, and continue the story. The same characters are now involved in totally different situations. One is a wealthy writer unknown to the others, several now run a detective agency. You will also see the people you met in "To Search and Prosper", all now also three years older. While attempting to solve a variety of mysteries, and as they travel around remember parts of the treasure trail solution. Depending on what has happened with the Treasure Trail this could help reveal the original or alternate solutions.

It will be fast moving, exciting, amusing and you will find the unexpected happens.

Order your copy now, and have it sent to you immediately on publication.

The page size and binding style will match this book. The number of pages is not yet known.

Order at today's prices £14.95 post free from:-

Knowledge Base Publications Ltd
19 Penybryn, Mountain Ash,
Mid Glamorgan CF45 3TJ

Or write and ask us to tell you when it is available.

CHAPTER TWO.

ARRIVAL.

He had just over two earth weeks to prepare, before being deposited on earth. In this time, he tried to get out of the mission, and studied as hard as he could, especially about the dangers.

In his briefing pack was details of an area which was at the junction of a number of militia areas or counties. This had been chosen so if one militia was after him he could escape into another area. Communication wise it was also good being a main railway crossroads. The area was well known to the Dagonites, as with a Roman road the area they had visited it many times since the time of the Romans. He learnt that religion was the centre of the humans life, of different religions, of dangers, of navigation skills and much more.

He had several special sessions to develop and tune his telepathic abilities. To do thought transmission between himself and humans, you treat them as you would an animal, he learnt, you use pictures not language.

He heard about language, dialects, and latin spoken by the church leaders and others who controlled the masses.

His name he was told, while on earth, would be Johannes, which is Latin for John a common earthling name. This was just in case he was captured.

He was told that humans have slow eyes, so if he kept moving, or just bounced on the spot he could not be seen, well probably wouldn't be seen. He learnt about cognitive overload, and how humans couldn't deal with lots of data at the same time, as their brains protected them, which was to his advantage, as they would shoot him if he did show. He learnt that there were some people who might see him, but this was not a problem as they had all been locked up.

The day came, and the large ship approached the earth, taking care not to go between the earth and sun, or it would create an eclipse. Using cloaking devices it could not be seen, and it flew over a junction on the old Roman road, before dropping 763 unceremoniously through the rubbish hatch. No one had even wished him good luck.

Within seconds the ship was gone. It was early summer, and around 4.30am earth time, there was no one around, and the light was soft.

It's cold enough to make you turn from pink to blue he thought as he stood looking at the sign by the crossroads. It doesn't make much sense.

He knew the way west went into Cow Honeybourne. He passed a lot more earthling homes than he expected, and found the centre of the village. Just past a large house with dead grass on the roof. Thatch he remembered it was called.

Oh dear, what had happened? Had there been a revolution? Had another race taken over the earth? Was all his learning out of date?

He approached the village church slowly. Had all order been destroyed? Did anarchy now prevail? Yes, the same up here.

What were all the lumps of hollow metal doing around. Were they some type of rubbish bin on wheels. He inspected one. Ford it said on it. Ah, that's it, a device for fording rivers. He inspected it further, but could not see how it would work, as it clearly was not totally waterproof from the bottom. Must just stand on it I suppose, he thought.

He quickly inspected the rest of the village. Found the place where all the horses were stored, but couldn't see any wagons.

He found a school, worked out the thatched building had to be a new centre for rituals. It had a sign saying 'Thatched Tavern'. He found another larger room, with no apparent use, labelled 'Village Hall'.

This was confusing. What was the church is now several houses, what was the chapel, it's now a printing place, and what was several thatched houses is now a new place of religion for Taverners.

He was inspecting the Tavern when he heard a noise, and saw a fording machine approaching at speed with a human trapped inside. The human was twisting a big wheel a bit one way, and a bit the other. Trying to get out I suppose, he thought.

It wasn't long before there were a number of these machines moving about. He saw people voluntarily go and climb into them, and some that managed to stop the machine and escaped. No horses or carts, just funny fording machines he thought.

Not knowing what else might have changed he set off across the fields to have a look at various types of trees and plants.

When evening came, and it started to get darker he returned to the village and approached the tavern. That's lucky he thought there's a ceremony going on inside. He watched.

Anarchy, everyone talking at once, lots of little groups. This is really unusual, he thought. He worked out it had to be something to do with the different coloured liquids in various shaped glasses that humans kept fetching.

It's no use I can't understand this place, he thought bouncing back. To his horror he realised there was a huge machine approaching him at speed, and he sensed that there were many bodies inside it. He bounced rapidly across the road into a side street and waited.

It was large and square shaped, and yes, it had a lot of horses inside it.

He was bouncing back into the road to have a better look at the machine, with the horses, when he realised behind him was another huge machine with big eyes shining.

He bounced as fast as he could. That machines not eating me, he thought. It won't get in there, he thought as he noticed an open door into one of the houses. As he bouncedthrough the door he nearly collided with several humans. He bounced up some wooden steps, and jumped over a fence, before hiding in a corner.

This is terrible, everything is not right here. If only I could get back to the ship, he thought as he rested in the corner of the cluttered room.

CHAPTER THREE.

FIEND OR FRIEND

Oh no, humans were coming up the wooden steps. The fence opened and a small blonde haired male human was put in. A boy, he thought. The boy looked straight at him. He bounced up and down, but the boy approached.
"Ha ha," the boy laughed. "Tick, tick."
Help the boy was attacking him, trying to dig his fingers in his neck. It didn't hurt though it was sort of pleasant. Lucky he isn't strong enough to tear me apart he thought.

At the sound of all the noise, he could hear three humans approaching. This time it was a young woman who entered. "It's okay mum," she called out, "Billy's just pretending to tickle empty space."
Empty space. I'm not empty space he thought, and then realised that she couldn't see him. Why could this boy?

As soon as the girl left he stopped bouncing, the boy had given him some tickles, a hug, a gentle sort of head bash, and was now pulling him over to a collection of toys on the floor. The boy had some model fording machines.
"Car.. car," the boy said. "Car... car."

Slower developing than I had been told, he thought, must be between four and six and has very little language yet. They had fun with the models, crashed them, pretended they could fly, stacking them up, and dropping them down a ramp on a model building when another human entered before he could start bouncing.
"Oh.. isn't he sweet," the girl said. "Does he have a name?" she asked the little boy.
"Bounce bounce," the little boy said.
"Oh. I think it needs a nick name, how about Jennifer."
"I'm not a Jennifer," 763 said. "You can call me Johannes."
"Oh good a talking toy," she said as she picked him up and immediately turned him upside down.

"It's good, I can't even see where the batteries go."
"Put me down."
"Oh that's good, must have a computer or something in it."
She sat him on the ground and pushed him over onto his side, then letting go to make him wobble.
"I'll call you Jo.... no I'll call you Hands, the girl said bending some of his fingers.
"Okay, I'm Hands," 763 said. "But don't hurt me."
"Sorry," the girl said. "My name is Cathy, and this is my special brother Billy."
"Oh hello," Hands said "I'm not a toy." The little girl inspected him. She looked all over him, turned him around, looked closely at this eyes. Made him open his mouth while she peered inside.
"Um... What are you?" Cathy asked.
"I'm a Dagonite.... A sort of visitor to this planet."
"E.T. Do you know E.T?"
"Who or what is E.T?"
"He's wrinkly, has a straight neck, a finger that lifts up and says E.T go home."
"No, not a Dagonite."
She was starting to look worried.
"E.T was children's friend, are you..... are you going to hurt us?"
"No, I want to be your friend."
She relaxed a little, but didn't seem quite sure.
"Okay," she said. "But what do you eat?"
"Anything wood like, what can you think of?"
She disappeared for a few minutes and reappeared with a packet of crisps.
"Any good?" she asked.
He tried one. "Very good.... um.... very good, what are they?"
"Pieces of potato, do you want to see a potato?"
"Oh yes please," this did taste really good he thought.
Within minutes Cathy was back with a middle sized potato.
"Um.." he said "about 200 grams, the packet says 26 grams."
"So," Cathy said looking a little confused.
"So this potato would make 8 bags of crisps."
"Goodness, I never realised that," she said staring at the dirty looking potato.
He took a bite of the potato. "Ahhh horrible."
Cathy laughed, and Billy copied, getting a little carried

away.
"You can't eat it like that. It has to be cooked."
He finished the bag of crisps. Really effective food conversion he thought, one potato makes eight packets of crisps. He folded the packet up carefully. A useful container this packet he thought.
"What do you use the packets for?" he asked.
"Nothing, we just throw them away."
"What, such waste, you could use it as plant pot, or reseal them and put a lot in a bag to make an air mattress or..."
Cathy interrupted, "rubbish, it's just rubbish," she took it from him, blew it up and clapped it between her hands making it go off with a bang.
What waste he thought, it's a good job they're not in space.

Cathy explained many things to him, she told of her older brother and sister, who were twins. Mandy was horrid all the time he learnt, and Bobby most of the time. She told him about her parents Alex and Sally, and about four grandparents. He wished he had taken more notice of the lectures, although he couldn't ever remember anyone explaining anything about six parents.

He learnt that tomorrow was a public holiday, as was the day after. That this was not unusual as every week had at least two public holidays. Some weeks he learnt had a lot more, and when they overlapped, you had to move some forward. It really was confusing.

If that wasn't bad enough. He learnt that some people work on public holidays, and their father, Alex, worked when he wanted to, so he would sometimes work everyday, and sometimes take a week or more off. Schooling was the same, two days off every week, lots of extra weeks, and some longer, even one holiday lasting six weeks. It really is surprising anything at all gets done, he thought.

The following day he stayed with either Billy or Cathy. Billy could see him all the time, but Cathy could only see him if he stopped bouncing. None of the other members of the family could see him as long as he kept moving.

Chapter Three

There was much he couldn't understand, like why Billy had a plastic thing around his neck when he ate, and shared his food with it, or why Sally the mother, was on a diet when she wasn't ill, or why Billy couldn't talk properly.

He had managed to get a good telepathic link with Billy, thinking in pictures, and found that Billy was used to this, as he already used a telepathic link to and from his father.

Sensory overload. That's what is wrong with Billy, he decided. As Billy was always laughing, smiling and the centre of attention he could see that there would be no advantage in trying to change things.

Billy liked to have him around, especially when he made the models move on their own or talk. All the models about 26 in all, were moving and Billy was squealing with excitement when Bobby, Billy's older brother walked in.

---- Sorry we have to leave it here ----

APPENDIX NINE.

OPENING TIMES FOR PLACES MENTIONED

BEDGEBURY NATIONAL PINETUM, Flimwell
East Sussex Telephone: 0580-211044
Open daily except Christmas Day - 10am to dusk.
Charges: £1.50 Adults, £1 OAP, 75p Children.

BENTLEY WILDFOWL AND MOTOR MUSEUM
Halland, East Sussex. Telephone: 0825-840573
HOUSE OPENS 1st April 1993.
Winter Months:
Open Weekends only 10.30am to 4pm last admissions.
Charges: £2.40 Adults and OAP's,
£1.50 children 4-15 years. Children under 4 FREE.
Family Ticket (2 adults and up to 4 children) £8.00
22nd March 1993 to 31st October 1993:
Open daily from 10.30am to 4.30pm last admission.
Charges: £3.40 Adults, £2.60 OAP's
£1.70 Children 4-15 years. Children under 4 FREE.
Family Ticket (2 Adults and up to 4 children) £9.00

THE TALES OF ROBIN HOOD, Maid Marian Way
Nottingham Telephone: 0602-483284
Open Daily except 24,25,26 December
2nd October to 3rd April: 10am to 3.30pm last admission
4th April to 1st October: 10am to 4.30pm last admission
Charges: £3.95 Adults
£2.95 children, OAP's and students.
Family Ticket (2 adults and up to 2 children) £10.95

IRONBRIDGE GORGE MUSEUM, Ironbridge
Shropshire Telephone: 0952-433522
Open Daily from March 10am to 5pm, June, July and August 10am to 6pm.
Some of the smaller sites may be closed during the winter months, telephone to check availability before your visit.
Charges: £7.80 Adults, £6.80 OAP's
£5.00 Children and students.
Family Ticket (2 Adults and up to 5 children) £23.50

GETTING ORGANISED

You may find it helpful:-

1. To extract all the things you are looking for onto cards for each place.

2. Working out where all the places are on a map so as to reduce travelling.

3. To use an Ordnance Survey Route Planning map which gives you a large view of the whole of the country.

4. To decode the section in Chapter Fifteen early, so that you know which clues you absolutely need for the solution.

5. To list the items you need to keep your eyes open for.

6. To make notes on each and every visit.

7. To carry this book with you wherever you go.

The more organised you are, the more likely you are to succeed.

People who do not solve the clues will be:-
People who don't look. (Stay at home or will get round to it somewhen).
People not organised.

You have the same chance as anyone else, being well organised will give you an advantage.